"If you want to take a shower . . ."
Jennie offered softly.

Stretching an arm along the back of the couch, Jake toyed with her braided hair. "Join me?" He could tell by the tension in her neck as his hand closed on it, rubbing softly, that his offer surprised her. "Oh, Jennie."

Their mouths tasted like hot coffee, but after a few moments she became aware of the dark masculine taste of him. Her hair was half braid, half loose, long tendrils skimming her cheeks, then his, as he pulled her down. No matter how she ordered her eyes to open, they wouldn't. Her body was too intent on sensations, the tug of his mouth, the feel of his cheek scraping hers when he kissed a trail along her neck from her ear to her sensitive collarbone. His hands were toughened by work, and the scratchy hard feel of him made her feel softer, more feminine. . . .

Suddenly, not gently, he took her mouth in a searing kiss. When she opened her eyes, she saw it, the look she feared—the look that came into his eyes that was more than fire, more than lust. . . .

WHAT ARE *LOVESWEPT* ROMANCES?

They are stories of true romance and touching emotion. We believe those two very important ingredients are constants in our highly sensual and very believable stories in the *LOVESWEPT* line. Our goal is to give you, the reader, stories of consistently high quality that may sometimes make you laugh, sometimes make you cry, but are always fresh and creative and contain many delightful surprises within their pages.

Most romance fans read an enormous number of books. Those they truly love, they keep. Others may be traded with friends and soon forgotten. We hope that each *LOVESWEPT* romance will be a treasure—a "keeper." We will always try to publish

LOVE STORIES YOU'LL NEVER FORGET
BY AUTHORS YOU'LL ALWAYS REMEMBER

The Editors

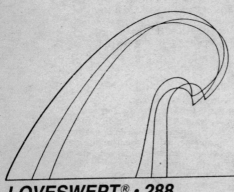

LOVESWEPT® • 288

Terry Lawrence
Where There's Smoke, There's Fire

 BANTAM BOOKS
TORONTO • NEW YORK • LONDON • SYDNEY • AUCKLAND

WHERE THERE'S SMOKE, THERE'S FIRE
A Bantam Book / November 1988

*If you would be interested in receiving protective vinyl
covers for your Loveswept books, please write to this address
for information:*

Loveswept
Bantam Books
P.O. Box 985
Hicksville, NY 11802

ISBN 0-553-21940-5

Published simultaneously in the United States and Canada

PRINTED IN THE UNITED STATES OF AMERICA

O   0 9 8 7 6 5 4 3 2 1

To Amy

One

He was knocking on her bedroom door. He'd tried the main door but had roused nobody. Then he'd walked down the long veranda, knocking on the next screen door he came to.

Inside was a bedroom, very plain, the whitewashed walls reflecting the faint light of morning. There was a dresser and a twin bed. A woman was sleeping on the bed, restlessly, in the nude.

He was knocking on her bedroom door. There was a hulking male presence, misty through the screen and her half-open eyes. The loose wooden doorframe rattled with each knock. The thin latch hook wobbled in response to his heavy hand.

Jennie thought how real dreams could be. She'd slept so badly, tossing and turning on damp sheets. It was so hot. Her hand slid over the crinkled cotton sheet that was spread around her bare legs, her fingertips noting every heat-pressed wrinkle. Why did this half-real man have to come knocking on her door, when all she wanted was sleep?

Her thoughts flitted like shadows on the adobe walls, which were meant to retain the night's coolness. But there had been no cool night for weeks, and her bedroom door stayed open, with only the screen in place. Jennie knew she had nothing to fear; she was safe on her ranch high in California's Inyo Mountains. The only people who had ever bothered her were a few bored teenagers from the little town below. No longer getting a rise out of her, they'd found somebody else to aggravate, another mountain valley to explore. So the door stayed open on hot nights, the screen latched against enterprising raccoons and lizards—not a man.

Jake Kramer banged on the door again, fighting the urge to frame his face with his hands and peer inside. It was barely dawn, but the woman he saw was no lonely fantasy, much as he would have liked her to be. The fact that she was real made him think too much, feel too much.

She'll probably kick my butt off this ranch the minute she wakes up, he thought, chuckling silently to himself. The sun was coming up behind him. He gallantly stepped aside and let the light slip in through the screen, casting the room in haze.

Her bare skin blushed soft and pink in the light, and there was a sheen of perspiration on her. Jake tilted his cowboy hat back and let out a long, silent whistle through his pursed lips. Maybe he was getting too lonely. Maybe it was only the light. He wiped the sweat off his lip with a fist; the day was warm already.

He watched the sheet fall in and out of her legs, draping over her thighs, dipping in the valley where they parted. She'd be angry when she woke up and realized he'd seen her. He chuckled again. He'd heard about her temper from the sheriff the night before, in town—and about her shotgun. But nobody'd warned him she looked so good. He'd seen the covers of her record albums, but it always was different meeting a celebrity in person.

"Yes, indeed," he said, his voice barely a whisper.

Her black hair curved in a trademark braid over her collarbone, the brushy end rising on the mound of one breast. The nipple was smooth and rosy, and she seemed to be eyeing him, her lids seductively half-closed in sleep, her lips curved slightly.

It looked as if she were smiling. A building throb told Jake it was a mighty inviting smile. His mind told him it was the angle. Either way he was tempted to open the screen and walk right in. He cleared his throat and brought his mind back to business.

"Jennie? Jennie Cisco?"

Jennie was awake, completely and utterly awake. Dreams didn't talk that loud. Their voices didn't echo off the adobe walls. She froze.

"Sheriff Kechnie sent me out this way. Sorry to disturb you, but you're on my list," he said.

List? she thought. She blinked rapidly, trying to get the grit out of her eyes.

"I'm here to notify the northern Cerro Gordo section."

She let out the breath she'd been holding and was immediately aware that the sheet that had felt like hot burlap during the night had been driven down to her hips by her restless thrashing. One leg had escaped the heat entirely and lay completely exposed on the edge of the bed.

She clutched the sheet, trying to tug it unnoticeably higher. How much could he see? she wondered. In the shadows she could make out the tight corner of his mouth. She couldn't tell whether he was grinning or not. He kept glancing away, as if the valley walls would close in on him any minute if he didn't keep an eye on them. He was being so obvious about not staring that Jennie knew he'd already seen plenty.

She considered the hideous option of lying there pretending nothing was happening while she inched the sheet higher and higher. "Ridiculous," she muttered, sitting up abruptly, pulling the sheet over her breasts in one movement. Her heart was still pounding rapidly. She was more startled than frightened. "Who are you?" she demanded.

"Sheriff Kechnie assigned me to this section."

He had a drawl of some kind, Jennie noted. Or maybe he was enjoying drawing this out.

"I'm to notify you that the fire in the hills northwest of this location . . ."

Jennie realized he had a piece of crumpled paper in his hand, not much more than a torn slice from a legal pad. He referred to it as he spoke. She used the opportunity to pull her leg in under the sheet.

". . . may be moving in this direction within the next thirty-six to forty-eight hours. Fire fighters will be moving in to try to contain it. However, you should be prepared to evacuate, should it become necessary." He lingered over the last four words, having had his say but not wanting to leave yet.

He wiped the sweat off his lip again. It was going to be another furnace of a day. The lack of breeze had kept the fire confined, but a series of hundred-degree days made him feel as if he were standing on the edge of the blaze even when it was twelve miles away. Jake found himself wondering how much cooler it would be in her nice, dark room.

With her in there, he knew it would be hotter.

"Miss Cisco?"

"I heard you," she said, her voice tight, carrying without effort to the door six feet from the foot of the bed. "I'm not evacuating."

"Problem," he said under his breath.

"What?" she asked sharply, her large brown eyes narrowing as she tried to distinguish his face through the screen and the shadows. She barely could tell if he was young or old—only that he was tall, and wide-shouldered. When he stood square in the doorway his shoulders were as wide as the screen.

He reached into his shirt pocket and pulled out a pencil. In his big hand it looked like a stub. He scribbled on the paper, turning it over and holding it against the doorframe as he wrote. The flimsy door creaked as he pressed on it.

Jennie was on her feet, holding the sheet in front of her. "What did you say?"

"If that fire comes this way you'll be a problem evacuee."

"Then you didn't hear me right. I won't be an *evacuee*." She enunciated every syllable with knifelike precision. "I'm staying right here."

"And hosing the place down with a garden hose?" He said it with such sarcasm, Jennie automatically tilted her chin in defense.

"If I have to." She flicked the braid over her shoulder. She was a fighter. With one major exception, there weren't too many things she'd wanted and hadn't gotten. Peace and quiet and to be left alone were the things she'd wanted most during the last two years. Her ranch was where she'd found that peace. She wouldn't leave it to someone else to save the place. She wouldn't trust anyone else.

He put the pencil and the folded paper in his pocket. With only the screen separating them, Jennie could see the way his plaid shirt stretched over his chest and hear him expel a deep breath. Whether it was a breath of exasperation or contemplation, she couldn't tell. She glared at him.

He was clearer now. Much. The early-morning light had grown enough to highlight the planes of his sturdy, angular face. Blue eyes. Laugh lines. Crinkles. His collar was open, revealing a small triangle of dark hair.

He didn't like the way she was looking at him. It wasn't coy or inviting. The fact that her eyes never left his face disturbed him—along with the effect her frank stare was having on his body. He didn't like that at all, not when the only things between them were a rickety screen door and the sheet she was holding just above her breasts. He took his hat off and wiped the sweat off his forehead, running a hand through his short sandy hair before putting his hat back on.

He couldn't stare back at her as boldly as she stared at him. It unnerved him to the point where he had to say something. "I've seen you before," he said.

The line was familiar. Jennie had heard it a thousand times in her career. She waited for the banality to ease the tension. It didn't. "I know who you are," he was saying, as if that put him one up on her. Considering what he'd seen minutes ago, and the soft tone of his voice, it was a much more intimate statement. She took it as an insulting reminder of how famous she'd *used* to be.

He leaned his hand on the wood frame of the screen door. It creaked. Jennie put hers on the other side, automatically, defensively. Her palm was damp against the painted wood. It was hot already. The night had never cooled down. Why didn't he just leave? she wondered.

"I'll be back," he said, looking directly into her eyes.

Jennie lifted the sheet a little higher. It had begun to sag in the center. Under the brim of his hat, Jake noticed her movement.

She splayed her fingers over the cleft. Years of voice control kept her tone steady in spite of the nerves that threatened to make it waver. "Don't bother coming back."

"No bother. It's my job." He touched his hat brim and nodded good-bye, but not before glancing over her shoulder. She followed his stare. Behind her, her full-length antique mirror presented the bare back view. Jennie suppressed a gasp and regally draped the wilted sheet around her. When she spoke her voice was low with anger.

"Now get off my porch and get off my land."

The contained violence in her voice kept Jake from grinning as he sauntered down the veranda and off the porch to the Jeep. It was a hard line to say, he thought, hard not to sound like a beleaguered woman in a western movie. But maybe that was how she saw herself, a self-sufficient prairie girl living in a fantasy western. Not the spoiled, well-known folk singer the people in town talked about. They were less proud of than perturbed by their famous neighbor, who refused to act neighborly.

"Suppose she can play any part she wants," he said to nobody as he started up the Jeep, shifted gears, and steered around the deep ruts on the winding mountain road leading from the ranch. But if she stayed or got in the way of fighting the fire, she'd be a problem. He chuckled again at the flash in her eyes when he'd caught sight of her in the mirror. Then he cleared his throat and shifted on the bumpy seat. For a problem she certainly was a lovely, womanly one.

He set his hat on the seat and stretched his head up above the windshield, letting the wind whip through his hair; the first breeze he'd felt all day. Going back over what had happened, he laughed aloud. She hadn't been about to let him in that door. He liked that. It kept things real simple when a woman knew her mind.

There was no hope of sleeping now, she realized. It was almost six-thirty. Jennie sighed, poured luke-warm water from the porcelain jug on the dresser into a basin, and splashed it on her face. It didn't help. She couldn't shake the idea of his gaze gliding over her skin as she'd slept, or the feeling of inti-macy that had connected them as they'd stood on either side of the screen. The only two people for miles . . .

Absently she rebraided her hair. Deep within she felt jittery and uneasy, like the dry, electric air hours before a thunderstorm. Her hands shook with a mild tremor.

"It's heat and nerves, that's all. And lack of sleep," she mumbled. She tugged on the jeans she'd left in a heap beside the bed and pulled on a plaid cotton shirt. Fresh from the dresser drawer, soft and thread-bare, it was cool against her hot skin.

He'd invaded her privacy, she thought, determined to complain to the sheriff next time she was in town. He'd shake his head and say he'd look into it, which was about all he ever did. Except when she'd bought the shotgun to deal with trespassers. Then he'd hightailed it directly up to the ranch to give her a lecture on responsible gun ownership—how to load it, clean it—especially how *not* to point it at anybody. Ever.

It had been the quickest response she'd ever gotten out of him. She had bought the gun at the general store at nine in the morning; he'd arrived at her ranch before lunchtime. She shook her head and smiled ruefully. That was how it was in a small town. News traveled fast.

So who was the man the sheriff had sent up that morning? she wondered. He actually seemed to care, as if he had some personal stake in her safety. To Jennie it only proved he wasn't a local. She knew their opinion of her. Caring didn't enter into it.

"That scrap of paper certainly didn't look very official." She shuddered. He could have been anybody. "Maybe I should be more cautious about locking the doors." She unlatched the screen, stepped onto the planks of the porch, and tossed the contents of the water basin onto the parched drive. She leaned against the textured adobe wall and sent her thoughts out to every corner of the ranch. It wasn't perfect, but she still needed to believe it was her ideal retreat. Even if she hadn't magically found what was missing in her life, it was better than the rat race her musical career had become.

Except for those rare occasions when she chose to sell a song or two, she'd dropped out completely. She knew people thought her legendary stage fright finally had won out. It had tormented her for years, but had never stopped her from performing, from reaching out to people through her songs. But just because a person writes sensitive songs doesn't mean she knows anything about real people's problems, Jennie thought wryly. That was where it had all gone wrong. She'd wanted to do more than sing; she'd wanted to help someone who idolized her and depended on her. The resulting failure had led her here. She'd stayed, insisting on her privacy and a ranch that was as safe and familiar as the old horse she was heading toward to saddle up.

Glaze. It was early for their morning ride, but she suspected he'd slept as little as she had lately. Believing in the innate sense animals possessed, she wondered if the far-off fire was making him jumpy too.

She strode across the crusty brown grass that led to the stalls at the end of the bunkhouse. The light seemed unusual this early in the morning—dim, dusty. Then again she wasn't used to being up at dawn.

Her boots scuffed over the straw scattered on the dirt floor. Crooning her good-mornings to the old gelding, she gently patted his neck. The horse stood, contented, as she slapped a blanket over his broad back and cinched a saddle around him.

"We're riding today, old friend. Let's go." She walked him past the corral, reminding herself again to paint the once-white rails.

"When it cools off," she promised herself, swinging a leg over the saddle. She settled into the rhythm of Glaze's steady lope as he found his way up the ridge and out of the valley—in the opposite direction that man had come from.

At the thought of him, she felt an immediate and unwelcome tightening in her stomach. He'd had such an intimate manner. Gentle. Insinuating. "You're imagining things," she scolded herself.

What had he said to make her feel he knew her more deeply than he possibly could? Was it the way the steady gaze of gray-blue eyes had held hers? He'd watched her naked and asleep; was that why she felt so vulnerable? She wasn't ashamed of her body, and sleeping nude in this heat was strictly using common sense. There was no need for her to feel embarrassed or . . . or violated. She shook her head as if rewriting a song lyric. Violated was the easy choice of a word, close, but not the right word. She didn't feel that way at all.

It was something in the way he'd looked at her. It hadn't been the superficial I-know-you of a fan, but a deeper look. He'd seen inside her. It was as if she'd been hiding in a dark room and he'd found her. The fact that that was literally what had happened didn't help. She tried to dismiss it as a chance encounter, but she couldn't.

With a "harumph," Glaze snorted as he stumbled over a stone and regained his footing. The path winding up the side of the valley was narrow, dense with trees, and littered with stones.

At the top of the ridge Jennie looked out over the government-owned land that surrounded her ranch. The Inyo Mountains. They were too far from L.A. or San Francisco to tempt weekend vacationers. Too barren, also, she admitted. And too desolate for a woman alone. She liked the feeling of being alone at the top of the world. She closed her eyes and inhaled deeply.

When she opened them, her gaze skimmed the peaks and valleys covered with scrub and pine. She focused on the spot where the fire burned. One peak was already charred black, the trees standing like matchsticks.

"Or a punk's spike haircut." Jennie liked the image. She didn't like the scene. The trees were black needles with no green undergrowth. Dense gray smoke masked flashes of red flame in the valleys. A heavy column of smoke rose into the sky, camouflaging the neighboring peak. Jennie followed the plume upward until it obscured the sun like a veil. That was when the hollow feeling in her stomach grew, and she realized why the light looked so strange now.

The fire had moved closer. She pictured what a stiff wind on a hot day could do and how fast it would travel through forests like tinder. She shuddered again.

The man had said be ready to evacuate.

Glaze shifted, and twisted his head, and Jennie listened to the dry pine needles crackle beneath his hooves. The least she could do was get him out of there. She patted his neck, absentmindedly scratching his mane. "I'll take you to Harbring's. They'll board you until this fire is under control."

She tugged the reins and turned him. A trickle of perspiration slipped from under her breast and glided to her waistband. She sat up straighter and wiped away the dampness. Her hand glanced over the thin cotton, and one nipple peaked. She thought of *him* again and forcefully shut him out of her mind.

She wanted her life neat, simple, uncomplicated. Any problems she'd handle on her own.

Maybe it was his job to issue warnings, to be Sheriff Kechnie's messenger. Underneath, Jennie told herself, he was just another curiosity seeker, who'd come up to the ranch with a better-than-average excuse.

"And he got a good look for his money."

She felt another trickle of sweat and a sudden awareness of the heavy undulating movement of the horse beneath her. Her thighs felt scratchy and confined by the denim of her jeans. Taking her mind off the heat, she promised herself a cool bath when she got back to the house.

Inhaling the rich smell of leather and horse sweat,

she urged Glaze into a faster walk down the winding trail and onto the valley floor. The horse kept walking. It was Jennie's heart that stopped.

A dozen men had arrived. They'd been there long enough to walk around but not long enough for the dust to settle. It hovered behind their trucks in the unmoving air. As far as she was concerned, they'd be off her property before it had a chance to come back down.

Her shout swept across the prairie grass and richocheted between the walls of the two bunkhouses like a rifle shot. *"Get off my land!"*

She dug her heels into Glaze's side, a motion the old horse was unaccustomed to. Prodded, he broke into an urgent gallop.

Obviously this was *his* fault. The yellow hard hats the men carried matched the yellow Jeep she'd seen that morning. *He* had to be behind this.

From a gallop Glaze slowed to an abrupt walk. Jolted, Jennie grabbed the saddle horn to stay on. The two of them always walked when they got to the corral, and the old horse knew it. Jennie gritted her teeth as one of the men snickered.

The men were milling around the entrances to the two bunkhouses, some taking shelter on the long verandas, out of the blistering sun.

Jennie dismounted, the lethargy she had been feeling suddenly replaced with sizzling energy. She tugged at the cinches and tossed Glaze's saddle to the ground. Only her fear of hurting him made her slow down to remove his bit. It hit the dust as fast as the saddle.

She slammed the corral gate behind her and walked down the dusty path between the bunkhouses, ignoring each man as she passed. There was only one man she wanted to see just then, and he wasn't in sight.

Jennie stopped in the small plot of land dividing the bunkhouses and put her hands on her hips. "All right, where is he?" she asked, her voice sharp and ringing.

The men traded looks, some leaning against porch posts, some toeing the dust. Finally one nodded his head toward the house.

Her house.

Two

"What! He's *in there*?" That did it! She was going to march into the house and—

Jennie whirled to see Jake leaning in the wide-open doorway, his shirt unbuttoned to the waist, sweat stains under his arms, a red bandanna tied loosely around his neck. This time there was no avoiding looking him up and down. From the wilted creases in his khaki slacks to the biceps revealed by short sleeves, Jennie felt the picture branded into her memory.

He looked blatantly masculine, casual, unassuming, and easy. So why did she feel so threatened?

Because he was in *her* doorway. And, dammit, she could tell he was going to stay there until *she* came to *him*.

Every man on the place was watching. Jennie felt the stir of butterflies in her stomach, like stage fright. Suddenly it was an effort to move, to banish the unreasonable fear that had haunted her through years of performing.

They're not an audience, she reminded herself,

they're intruders. And the sooner she got rid of their boss, the sooner they'd take their eyes off her and leave, she realized.

Her boots scuffed the dust and crunched on pebbles as she walked. She concentrated on putting one foot in front of the other and nothing more, not the man in front of her, not the drops of sweat making her shirt stick in places she didn't want it to stick.

Jake thought she looked just as good in clothes. The jeans fit her like skin; her black hair flashed in the sun. He was looking forward to hearing what she had to say. He knew it would be a mouthful. A grin he couldn't suppress teased the corners of his mouth.

Jennie stopped at the bottom of the porch stairs, her voice husky and parched. "You got any authorization to be on my land? I'd better see a paper. Now."

The twinkle in his eyes made her resolve stronger.

Jennie raised her voice, gesturing at the group of men behind her while never taking her gaze from his. "You get every one of these men off my place! You've got no right—"

"My right's on the kitchen table," Jake said. With that he turned and walked into the house, the screen door slamming behind him.

Jennie muttered a couple of choice words and barged in behind him, swinging the screen so wide it banged against the house and bounced back, almost swatting her on the rear.

The house was pitch-black to her after being in the bright sun, but she knew her way through the open living room and around the massive stone fireplace. She turned into the kitchen and there he stood, appearing comfortable and at home, sipping a lemonade and contemplating a much-folded piece of paper, which she snatched from his offering hand. He took another sip of lemonade.

She swallowed the dust from her ride, unwillingly noting how small the glass looked in his large hand. She commanded herself not to listen to the ice tinkling, or think how good the water droplets looked on the outside of the glass.

She tore her glance away from him when he licked his lips, and cursed the infuriatingly satisfied expression on his face. She concentrated on the paper. It had a seal. It had been duly signed and sworn. Hell, she thought, they'd even gotten it notarized. But it said nothing specific.

She flicked her braid over her shoulder with one hand and fixed a level brown-eyed gaze on the man who was six inches taller and a good seventy-five pounds heavier than she. She'd never considered herself frail, and sheer size didn't intimidate her. She stared at him long enough to get that point across to him.

What she didn't want him to know was that legal gobbledygook made her blood run cold. She'd wrangled with enough shifty managers and promoters in the past, all with a lawyer and a paper on their side. "So?"

"You want to know what it means?"

His voice was soft. She remembered that intimate tone. She'd been hearing it ever since they'd met, saying her name, warning her, teasing her—no, it was his eyes that teased. His voice was smooth, low, and direct. And direct was something Jennie could deal with.

"Okay, I do want to know."

"It means I've been deputized, *authorized*, by the National Forest Service, the town council, the sheriff, and any other authority you want me to get a paper from, saying I can set my group up here to fight this fire."

"What fire? It's twenty miles away." Her voice was flat, her eyes unresponsive.

"Twelve as the crow flies. Don't let the valleys fool you."

It wasn't the valleys she was worried about. His eyes were blue and friendly and very sincere.

"I don't want trouble, Miss Cisco. I'm here to help."

" 'I'm from the government and I'm here to help.' Isn't that one of the three most common lines? Along with 'The check is in the mail,' and 'I'll still respect you in the morning'?"

"You think I don't respect you after this morning?"

Her eyes flashed more brightly that any blaze, and she grabbed the glass of lemonade from his hand. It was incredibly rude of her, and for a moment she didn't know what to do with it. She set it on the table with a thump. "Out!"

Jake chuckled and took a step back. It wasn't a retreat; it just gave him a better look at the spitfire who had a notion about fighting a raging brush fire with a garden hose. He had the immediate thought that if circumstances came down to it, that was exactly what she'd do.

Her hair was braided in a coal-black braid; her eyes were a rich caramel-brown color. There was a dew of perspiration at the base of her throat, where her pulse beat hard, and her blouse was unfastened four buttons down, just baring the swelling of her small breasts. It was nothing compared to what he'd seen that morning, but somehow it was even more tantalizing.

Her shirt was unbuttoned, and Jennie knew it. She felt it every time she took an angry breath. Charging across the yard after her hot ride, she'd never gotten around to buttoning it. There was no way she was going to give him the satisfaction of doing it now, not even when the perspiration mingling with the air made her nipples tighten to chilled peaks. Compared to the heat of her body, all it took was a slight breeze, a breath of air, and she felt a shiver course over her skin.

Air?

It was him! His lips weren't pursed in consternation; they were forming a silent whistle so he could blow downward. The breeze was him, and he knew where he was pointing it.

Trapped by her own stubbornness and his sheer audacity, Jennie couldn't move. She glared into his eyes, eyes surrounded by fine wrinkles etched into his tan. He was practically daring her to do something about it.

She tore her gaze away from his, but it escaped no farther than his mouth, noticing for the first time that lips pursed to whistle were also pursed to kiss.

Jennie backed against the table, her hand gripping the glass of lemonade. She was tempted to toss it right where it would cool him off.

"Whoa," Jake said with a laugh, stepping back and breaking the spell. That was more like it. For a moment he thought he'd caught an emotion softening her glare, something besides anger.

Jennie set the glass on the table. She'd won, but he'd known what she was thinking before she'd made a move, and that unnerved her. Her physical reaction to him unsettled her even more.

He picked his hat up from the table, twirling it nervously in his hands. "I've got eleven men on this site and a dozen setting up on the northeast perimeter. We're going to fight the fire. If it moves this way, we'll do what we can to stop it."

"I'll fight it myself," she said, wondering why it was such an effort to sound angry, when she had every right to be furious. "I've told you before this is my land—"

"And thirty yards down the valley is state land. The former owner used it for grazing, and there's an old chicken coop on it. I'd rather my men bedded down in real bunkhouses, and you've got two standing empty."

"I don't care where you or your men bed down. I want you out." The edge was back in her voice.

"I heard you." His voice was still soft, intimate; his eyes shaded and downcast.

"So do it!"

Jake set his jaw, took one step forward, and tugged her to him with one strong arm around her waist. Pressed in tight, his body made it clear she hadn't been the only one affected a moment before. "Don't tempt me, lady."

He let her go so fast, her heels thudded on the floor, and she swayed.

Jennie blushed a furious red, the color rising under her olive complexion. Did he think she was leading him on? Did he think her blouse had been unbuttoned on purpose? She'd never expected him to be there when she got back from her ride. Never expected to see him again. How dare he . . . ?

Jake thought he'd never seen a woman more beautiful. The spark in her eyes, the flush on her cheeks— the passion. The roller coaster of sensations came flooding back. He had to get away before he did something he'd never live down—like kiss her.

He turned on his boot heel and stalked out of the kitchen.

He was leaving at last. Jennie tried to savor her hollow victory. "And stay out!" she called after him. "You can find yourself another camp."

He kept walking, his boots sounding loud on the wooden floor.

Jennie stood beside the stone fireplace. "I don't need you. Or your help," she added lamely and a little late.

"There's just no talking to some people. Good day, Miss Cisco. By the way—"

He stopped at the screen door and looked back over his shoulder. For a moment Jennie thought he was going to come back. Her heart almost stopped.

"My name is Jake," he said, "Jake Kramer." He pushed the screen door open with the flat of his hand and walked out.

"Of all the—" she started to say, but was drawn to the door. She watched him walk, his lean hips moving with each stride, challenging, in an utterly masculine way. He didn't push it; he laid back. He'd let her come to him.

"You wish," she muttered. She plopped herself down on the sofa and stared at the empty black hole of the fireplace. On such a hot day it was hard to imagine ever being cold enough to cozy up to a fire.

Deep down, the reasonable part of her was glad the fire fighters had picked her land to camp on. What better protection could she have? The generous part of her would have insisted they use the bunkhouses if they'd pitched so much as a pup tent anywhere else. Their boss was right.

He was also the main problem. Not only did he have the gall to do all this without her permission, not to mention making himself at home in her kitchen, but he had the audacity to pretend to care. And just being near him threatened to awake a part of her she wanted left undisturbed.

So she reacted with anger. Her tough front cloaked a woman set loose in the music world at the age of

seventeen, who had learned fast to cultivate a reputation for temper. Not many people got past her
moat—only those she chose to let in.

She punched a pillow. All she'd ever wanted was
to sing, to make some kind of mark, to reach people,
touch someone with her music. That someone had
been Karen.

Jennie had had so many big ideas back then. She
called the ranch *El Dobro*, after her favorite guitar.
It was her haven, their haven. She had vowed to get
Karen off drugs and out of the backstage meat market her friend's vulnerability had drawn her to. But
it had never been enough.

"Maybe I wasn't enough," she said thoughtfully.
Letting her head fall back, she took a deep breath.
"Stop kicking yourself. It's over." The ranch was all
she had left. Two years had drifted by, and she had
no intention of leaving. What had started as a temporary retreat had turned into a life away from music. It wasn't a whole life, but if she didn't push it,
the seams didn't show.

Until people invaded, their presence starting Jennie on a long list of unasked, unanswered questions
about loneliness and reaching out and good inten-
tions. Responsibility. Guilt. It was a long list, and
right now she was too damn tired to drag herself
through the coals all over again.

She stretched out her legs, boots hanging over the
arm of the couch, and lazily lifted her head once to
check on Glaze. He was standing in the shade of the
one tree in the paddock. She was exhausted. The
dust itched under her eyelids. She reminded herself
she'd have to see to Glaze, but before she could do
anything about it, she was drifting off, her fuzzy
thoughts repeating themselves like the chorus of a
song.

Fire fighters didn't bother her, but she didn't want *him* around. He set her nerves, her skin, her teeth on edge. She'd reacted so strongly, but why? Why him?

Jake tossed his hat on the cot in the one private room the bunkhouse had to offer and unrolled a sleeping bag he knew would be too hot to sleep on. Sleeping nude might not be a bad idea. He wondered if Jennie would.

He heard the scrape of a crate in the next room, the sound of men moving into both bunkhouses. In case she caused a fuss, he had his argument ready. She'd said "I don't care where you or your men bed down." As far as he was concerned, that was permission. He wasn't about to have his men pitching tents thirty yards away, when perfectly good, albeit rundown, buildings were at hand. They had enough hard work in front of them, and he'd do what he could to make it easier on them. If Miss High-and-Mighty didn't like it, she could sue him.

He'd seen a lot of her that day—and had felt her in his arms for one shocking second. Very suave, he thought; crush her waist in one lunging grab, then drop her.

But he couldn't forget how she'd felt in his arms: fragile but full of spirit. He could still feel the heat of her skin radiating through her shirt, her ribs expanding in the circle of his arm as she took a startled breath.

His smile faded. Maybe keeping her at arm's length from now on would be a better idea. He knew damn well it would be.

•   •   •

After the local Forest Service agent gave them a rundown on the local terrain and his experience with similar fires, the men settled down. The afternoon stretched out in front of them. Some of them tried to lighten the mood. After a couple of dud jokes they realized Jake was in no mood for levity.

Heeding his curt commands, they fell into a well-drilled regimen of stowing their gear and getting the fire-fighting equipment cleaned and ready for the upcoming battle with the blaze. The talk dropped to a low murmur.

Later in the evening Jake sat in a corner of the bunkhouse porch rubbing carbon deposits off a rubber coat, the result of pine smoke in Idaho on their previous assignment.

"You're gonna rub the finish right off that." Chick, one of his crew, sat down beside him with a heavy sigh befitting a man twenty years older than most of the fire fighters.

"It's a mess."

Chick shrugged. No comment was needed. Jake looked up, glanced at the main house, and shook his head in disgust. So far she was letting them stay. Why wasn't he pleased instead of being so damned antsy. He'd wanted her to argue. It was easier that way. When a woman knew her mind and you weren't in it, she set you straight and you went on your way.

Safer, he thought. No involvement. No hurt. None of the sudden need that sneaked up on him when he remembered holding her. Not simply the physical need for a woman; there was more to the feeling, and it scared him. Getting involved with her would mean more to him than a casual encounter.

"Damn." He was disgusted with the whole day.

"Jake?"

"Yeah?"

One of the men was toeing the edge of the porch. "Bad news."

"Uh-huh." Jake waited until the man was ready to go on. There was no sense running after more bad news, he decided.

"Joey left a load of supplies behind."

"Behind?" Jake squinted up.

"In town. We're gonna have to go back."

Jake thought for a minute. She'd probably see a truck drive away and think they were leaving. Maybe she'd lighten up. Jake spit on the dust. Why did he care what she thought? "So go. We're not going to be doing much tonight anyway. Tomorrow we'll make our first try."

The man sidled away. Chick whistled tunelessly to himself. He rubbed his cheek with the backs of his fingers.

"So what's your beef, Chick?"

"Ain't mine."

"No? You've been sitting here twenty minutes."

"Doin' no work and gettin' paid for it."

"That's not my problem. You work as hard as anybody, and if you want to sit when nothing's going on, be my guest."

"Very free of you."

"Just don't ever sit down at a fire."

"You know I wouldn't," the older man said quietly.

Jake cringed. He knew it. It wasn't Chick's fault he was so testy. "Sorry, Chick. Must be the heat. Making me edgy."

"She'd make any man edgy."

Jake looked at him sideways; Chick's lined face didn't move. Was he talking about the lady or the day? he wondered, then let the thought go.

The truck rumbled into life and lifted a cloud of

dust behind it as it headed down the drive. It back-fired once. Jake jumped, then silently cursed himself for his nerves.

He'd felt like dry tinder since dawn.

One of the men called out from the other bunkhouse. "Chick! You breaking in the seat of those jeans, or are you gonna come help us with these crates?"

"All right, all right. What say we get a card game going, Jake? Poker?"

"Sorry, I've got the computer to set up. I want to feed in some information on the conditions. Think I'll turn in early." He didn't know how he'd sleep in this heat. There wasn't a cool breeze for miles. "Don't keep 'em up too late."

"Don't have that much money on me. Besides, we got a fire to fight in the morning."

Finally the sun was starting to sink, making a dusky mist that reminded Jake of the morning's dawn. The real fire had started then, in his belly, in his gut.

Three

Jake tilted himself back in his chair on the porch and let his hat shade his eyes. Under the brim of his hat, he could watch the house. The heat weighed down on him as if he were in a sauna. The fresh shirt he'd put on was unbuttoned as far as it would go. Nothing was going to help.

She'd started picking out a tune on the piano a while back. It was all Jake could do not to drop everything and listen. It was a melody she went over and over, changing notes here and there, and every time making it better. He waited for her voice, wondering what words she would add. The playing stopped. The house was quiet.

Was she in the kitchen now? Did she glance out the window his way when she passed? The house had a pitched roof and, from what he'd seen inside, a loft for a bedroom. Heat would rise and collect there. He didn't wonder that she slept in the bedroom off the porch. But would she sleep there now, in a room with nothing but a screen door? He doubted it.

Nothing moved. The heat shimmered.

Jake shifted and cursed. He might as well get some work done. Ever since the meeting with the local ranger he'd been ready to get down to his specialty, plotting the course of fires with a computer and his own personalized programs.

He cleared away the packing box and stretched below the table to plug in the monitor. There was no electricity. He kicked the cot away from the wall, then stalked angrily through the bunkhouse, trying every outlet.

Jake lost what was left of his temper. The witch! She'd turned off the power!

He had important work to do. Brush fires could flare dangerously and wildly with any gust of wind. He and his men had to be prepared for any contingency. Lives were at stake.

Jake stomped straight to the main house. His boots banged on the porch and his fist rattled the door.

"Cisco!"

Jennie jumped up from the piano, freshly written sheets of music fluttering to the floor.

"Lady, you don't know who you're playing with. Get that electricity back on! Now!"

Jennie held her ground by the mahogany baby grand and folded her arms, determined not to quail before the large man standing inside her door. "To the bunkhouses?" Her eyes widened for emphasis. "I'm sorry, but there isn't any."

"Don't give me that. There are outlets." He stepped menacingly closer.

"I had it disconnected when I bought the ranch. I only need the stalls heated in the winter for Glaze, and I use a generator for that. Otherwise, no power. Sorry." Her voice was so easy and lilting, her air of victory so serene, Jake wanted to strangle her. He didn't know the effort she was putting into her performance. "Now, if you'd like to share a stall with Glaze . . ."

He would have liked to get his hands on her swanlike neck, which arced when she looked up at him. But the thought of how smooth her skin would feel and the way the vein would pulse under his touch stopped him cold.

He stepped back and muttered to himself, his look no less black, though the tide of his thoughts had turned. She was like the moon—white and pale—and she made men do crazy things. He wiped his bandanna across his brow. "We need electricity."

"It'd take days to hook it back up. You'd need an electrician. They'd have to string a line."

"We need power. I've got to use my computer."

"Really," Jennie said, conveying as little interest as possible. "And why, may I ask?"

"I'm a fire-behavior specialist. I calculate terrain type, wind patterns, vegetation, precipitation, all of which require customized computer programs."

Jennie interrupted him as he bit off each word. "What do you do when you're out in the field?"

"I take one with batteries. I was told there'd be electricity," he said, as if it were her fault.

"Then maybe you'll have to move someplace else. I do hope your men find better accommodations elsewhere, but I'm no electrician, and I can't hook up the bunkhouse."

Jake glanced cursorily around the living room. "You won't have to."

None too gently ripping the cord from the useless outlet, Jake carted the computer up to the house.

Maybe if he worked fast enough he wouldn't have time to think why it was so urgent that he look at his programs that night, when portable generators or his battery-operated computer could be shipped fast.

It was the damn look of triumph on her face, the "I knew I'd be right in the end" expression he couldn't stand. Didn't the woman know they were there to help her, maybe to save her ranch? Didn't she know she needed them a hell of a lot more than they needed her?

Her hostility and invulnerability were just an act. Jake knew it as surely as he knew what size boot he wore. Underneath it all she was as needy and lonely as anybody. . . .

His hands full, Jake kicked the screen door open. He set the computer on the kitchen table, ignoring Jennie's ineffectual, often colorful language. Her arms flew out in all directions, her pointing finger jabbing at him like a darting bird. Jake imagined her strumming a guitar with those hands. She'd balled them into fists now, clenched and tight like her jaw. Realizing she wasn't getting anywhere, her tirade stopped. Her wide, full mouth was drawn in a tight line.

He muttered as he dragged the table closer to the wall from the middle of the room, so the cord would reach. It scraped across the Spanish tile.

"Be careful!" she said.

Jake barely hid a smile. She wasn't afraid of anything, was she? She was tough as nails when she wanted to be, yet in the few hours he'd known her, he could have sworn there were traces of some other emotion—a softness, a vulnerability. Did she ever want to feel something besides anger? To be held?

He squelched his thoughts, setting his hat firmly on the table.

Jennie paced the kitchen like a mountain lion, scanning the cooking implements that hung from nails on the walls, looking for a lethal weapon. It was bad enough he'd moved onto her land; there was no way he was moving into her house.

Obviously, he already had.

Jake sat and stretched his legs under the table until his dusty heels found a resting place on the seat of the chair opposite him. He flipped a switch, and the computer purred. He ran a hand over the stubble on his cheek and typed in a few numbers, pecking a letter at a time, calling up files. For someone engrossed in his work, he never missed a movement she made or a mutinous look she threw his way. He was enjoying himself. No amount of peering at the screen could hide the grin he kept wiping away with his bandanna.

To Jennie his concentration became a new rule, one meant to be broken.

She opened the refrigerator, intent on finding something loud to crunch on—carrots, an apple. The cool air flooded over her, and she was overcome by the sheer pleasure of it whispering against her skin. She surreptitiously opened a button on her shirt and let the coolness touch her a little lower. As the steam of cold air floated past, an unintentional sigh escaped her lips.

The clicking of the computer keys stopped. Jennie opened her eyes. She hadn't meant to be the distraction. She grabbed a bright blue pitcher of lemonade and two jangling metal ice-cube trays from the freezer. The trays clattered into the sink. The refrigerator door closed with a whoosh and a thud, the best it could do in the noise department, she supposed.

Jennie flicked her braid over her shoulder and used the opportunity to glance at Jake. He was back at work.

Fine, she thought, let him not notice. She turned the water on full blast, banging the trays against the ancient porcelain sink, plunking the cubes into a glass one by one. She poured the lemonade slowly; the sound of the splash itself was refreshing.

All he did was click away. Her antique Regulator clock ticked. The long-drawn-out summer evening began to take on the overtones of a nightmare. How long was he going to sit there?

Jennie left the sink and roughly pulled out a kitchen chair on the opposite side of the table. Jake's boots hit the floor. "Oops."

"No problem," he muttered, peering more closely at the amber letters on the screen.

Jennie let the lemonade slide down her throat, sighing for all she was worth. She had a definite advantage in the heat. Except he was the one who'd taken over her house. And her land. "So what do you know about computers?"

"Everything I can teach myself."

"Must not be much."

Jake chuckled and pecked at a few more keys. "It does what I need it to. With modifications."

"Do 'em yourself?"

"Sure. Right now I'm calling up locations of asbestos forests."

"Asbestos?"

"A nickname for concentrations of dense vegetation, mostly lodgepole pines in this area. They don't burn easily, and sometimes they'll stop a fire in its path long enough for us to put it out. I'll be collecting information in the field tomorrow to add to the data base."

"Oh. So you're a computer freak, huh?"

He looked at her directly. This man was no freak. Certainly no computer nerd with thick glasses, she decided. He looked like he'd just ridden in off the range and sat himself down at the bar for a beer. Now he needed a willing saloon girl to pull onto his lap.

Fat chance, she thought.

Jennie took another sip and felt a twinge of guilt at being so rude as not to offer him a glass of lemonade. She didn't let it get her up from the table. "So where are you from?"

"Missouri."

"Really." She sounded completely disinterested.

"Where are you from?"

"Minnesota. Isn't anybody out here from California?"

He chuckled softly, a sound she was surprised she liked. A corner of her mouth turned up in a smile.

"Yeah." She sighed. "It never got this hot back home."

"We had hot spells in Missouri. Of course, we never got snow like in Minnesota."

For some reason the small talk relaxed her. She found herself wanting to compare notes, the more mundane the subject the better. Weather was a safe topic, the winters she'd seen, the difference between Minneapolis and a small town like Lone Pine, where she did her shopping.

She hadn't chatted in ages, afraid the people down in town would be curious, or nosy, or disapproving. Going into Lone Pine was almost like battling stage fright. She handled both the same way—she avoided them. "What town in Missouri?"

"A little place, probably not even on the map. Population two hundred, a hundred and twenty miles north of Kansas City. Haven't lived there since I was twenty."

"And when was that?"

"About twelve years ago. I've lived in Montana since."

"Montana, huh?" She'd written a song about it once, her biggest hit.

Jennie considered telling him about it. It would keep him from his work. But he wasn't getting annoyed. He seemed as pleased to have someone to talk with as she did. "So what brings you to California?"

"The fire."

Jennie wanted to know what kind of man followed fires from state to state. It couldn't be much of a life; nothing settled, no real home. Kind of like touring, she guessed.

She watched him for a minute, noting that his eyes were suddenly serious. In the fading light his blue irises were wide and dark. Jennie lost track of how long she looked into them.

"Then you won't be around long," she murmured with a tone of finality. She didn't know if she should be happy or disappointed, although for reasons she didn't understand, she didn't feel much triumph at the thought of ultimately getting rid of him.

He shrugged. His big shoulders showed on either side of the computer screen. A tan shirt stretched on a muscular chest with three buttons undone, no undershirt, and a few fine golden hairs—Jennie noticed. She wondered if he noticed her fingertips tightening on her glass.

Jake watched her round brown eyes look to the

glass, the back of the computer, then back up to him.

"You married, Jake?" Jennie asked casually. She'd always known how to control her voice, but her darting eyes gave something away.

"Was. And you?"

"Don't you know about me?"

"I know you were famous."

"Past tense."

"You've been away."

"I've stayed away. I don't want that anymore."

"What is *that*?"

"Tours," she said quickly. Then she thought and gave him a more honest answer. "Responsibilities. Being crowded. Fans."

"You don't like 'em?"

"They're great. But some of them take the music too seriously. Every lyric means something to them. You feel responsible after a while."

"What they believe isn't your fault."

She gave him credit for having some sensitivity. "No. The temptation is when you start thinking they're right. With all those 'marvelous insights into human nature and the ways of love,' " she said, quoting from an old review, "you begin to believe that what you say or sing can really help people. A fatal mistake."

She took another sip. She wasn't looking at him anymore, but at a space somewhere inside the grain of the plank table, a place in the past. "I wanted to help people."

"Never would have guessed," he muttered.

She laughed, but her smile vanished quickly as she absently played with the end of her braid. She pulled off the rubber band and unwound her hair halfway, rebraiding it as she talked. "I'm a sucker for a sob story—was, that is. You can't be naïve for long in this business. There are people waiting to exploit your every weakness. I'll never be that gullible again."

He wondered if it was a man who'd made the once-soft woman hard. Suddenly, irrationally, he felt like apologizing for the whole male sex. He pulled himself up short. Whatever rocky road had led her to this ranch was her business, and hers alone. He wasn't going to get involved.

She looked at him sharply then, and Jake had to tear his gaze away from the motions of her fingers twining in her hair. "When you realize you can't even help yourself, much less your fans, it brings you back to earth fast. Don't you just love singers who have opinions on every issue? All ego. I was lucky; I got out before anyone found out what a fake I was."

Jake watched the thick black strands of hair intermingle as she talked, the kinked waves being put back in place. She would look magnificent with her raven-black hair wild around her oval face. He pictured her lying down, her head on a pillow, hair spread in disarray. It made a stark, heat-producing picture. He reminded himself she hadn't worn it loose earlier that morning. She'd had it braided even as she slept, no doubt because of the heat.

"I don't want a singing career anymore." With that she snapped the rubber band back in place.

"You still write music."

She stared at him, startled.

"How could I help hearing? I was right outside."

"Yeah." It was a bald reminder that, for all the land surrounding her, she wasn't alone anymore.

The conversation slowed, and their gazes locked. Jennie couldn't shake the awareness of how close he was—two or three feet away, with his boot near her bare foot under the table. She was aware of the thickness of his muscled arms in the short sleeves of his work shirt, aware of the smell of a man that pervaded her senses so subtly, she wasn't sure if she imagined it.

One thing she couldn't deny. The keenness of his blue eyes cut through every defense she'd put up since she'd met him, pinning her to the spot like a doe caught in headlights. He'd be sleeping in the bunkhouse that night. He was in her kitchen at the moment. He might be around for days. Then he'd be gone.

The moment lingered. Time slowed. Neither of them missed what was happening. He looked away, but contact wasn't broken. His large hands rested on the table on either side of the keyboard. He leaned forward as she leaned back. She thought he was reaching for her, but he took the lemonade instead.

Jake drank from her glass, his Adam's apple bobbing as he swallowed. He savored the cold liquid all the way down. He handed back the glass, knowing even when his eyes had been closed she'd never stopped watching him. He licked his lips.

The glass sat on the table between them. Jake slid it in small circles in the pool of moisture he'd lifted it from.

They were quiet, contemplating each other. He offered it to her, and she drank the rest, her gaze on his until the coolness hit her deep.

What was she going to do? She'd let him in, they'd talked, they'd shared. He'd be leaving in a matter of days. Jennie got up and tossed the ice cubes in the sink.

"I have to see to Glaze for the night. How much longer do you have to work on that thing?"

Jake glanced at the screen, the cursor blinking at him like reality. He knew she was right to pull away. He was letting her set all the limits. Somewhere along the line he'd messed up, and he didn't know how. Half of him wanted her so much, it hurt like a kick in the gut. The other half wanted her to keep the lines drawn and make sure he stayed within them. From what he'd seen, she was strong enough to do that. Suddenly he knew he wasn't.

He watched her as she stood at the sink making another pitcher of lemonade. Her jeans were faded and soft, creases underlining where the roundness of her buttocks filled them out. She was womanly, even in the nondescript plaid shirt.

He stood and walked toward her, placing his hands on her waist. It was small and delicate under her mannish clothes. Her sharp intake of breath made her ribs expand at his touch. He didn't have to turn her. She turned automatically, her lips parted in protest. All he heard was a breathy, inarticulate gasp. All he saw was her round brown eyes widening as he brought his mouth down on hers. He slid in closer, rasping his shirt against hers, teasing nipples that were already taut against the cotton nap of the fabric.

His lips brushed hers, and he waited for an argument, a slap. It didn't come. Her lips were still parted. He felt the eddies of breath between them, and stemmed it with his open mouth.

Too shocked to move, Jennie felt the pull of his kiss, the first explorations of his tongue. A groan caught in her throat.

Jake lifted his head, daring to open his eyes, expecting to see her fury. He saw confusion, silence, denial, and need. A voice in his head said she wasn't going to stop him. His body was taking the lead. It was a language they both spoke hesitatingly, as if they were exiles returning home.

They were lonely people. Jennie appeared to deny it. Jake accepted it as a given in his life. Emotional contact was rare; relationships wary and superficial.

Jennie's lips were dry. Jake moistened them with his tongue, and she let him in. She was no longer aware of his body pressing hers, but of hers meeting him, her hands sliding up his arms, encircling his broad back, clenching shoulder blades that moved as his arms came around her waist to meld her to him.

Curiosity, Jennie thought, that was what it was— the scary, irresistible emotion that had seized her the moment he'd touched her. Curiosity made her stand and feel and experience how he moved, how her limbs became leaden and restless all at once. All evening she'd been curious about how he would feel in her arms, doing what he was doing now, the man who had walked into her dream that morning and refused to leave.

Their mouths separated. A soft growl of satisfaction from low in Jake's throat brought Jennie around. She opened her eyes. He was curious too, she told herself, but the thought did little to squelch the sensations fluttering inside her like startled caged birds. Her body stiffened, and she realized how thoroughly she had formed herself to him. No wonder he was so pleased with himself.

She twisted in his hands and backed up hard against the sink. The edge of it hit her in the back. "Ow!"

Jake smiled a sly, ingenuous cowboy's smile. He licked his lips. "Now, don't tell me that hurt."

Jennie glared at him, finding the best way to hide her embarrassment was to get angry. How could she have capitulated so easily? He'd taken over the house, the ranch, and now she was giving him everything else!

Jake didn't need to hear her say the words. Just as their kiss had been silent, so was her order to leave. He turned and walked around the table, laughed quietly, and shook his head.

Was he laughing at her? she wondered. Jennie straightened. Lord, what was she? A tease? A desperate woman? Two years without a man, and all it took was one kiss? She flushed and agitatedly brushed away a stray curl that stuck to the perspiration on her forehead.

Jake pretended not to notice. He was punching the keys on his computer, shutting it down. He extracted the diskette, bluntly hit the off switch, and pulled the plug. He considered thanking her for the use of her electricity, but didn't want something thrown at him. Well, he thought, he'd gotten her to tell him off, even if it wasn't in so many words.

He looked up again. She was still glaring at him. Now go back where you belong, she seemed to be saying.

It wasn't as easy as that. If it had been, he could have looked her straight in the eye. She really hadn't told him off. She'd responded willingly, unmistakably.

Jake put on his hat and nodded, leaving Jennie standing where she was.

The next day passed quietly. Jennie was half awake, listening to the trucks leave before dawn, men's voices muttering and calling in the half-light. Equipment was loaded with bangs and thuds on the pickup beds. By the time she awoke again it was morning. The ranch had been left to her and Glaze.

She tried to stick to her routine, banishing as quickly as it arose every thought of Jake, every examination of her own conduct the previous night. There'd be time enough for that when he was gone and life was back to normal. Maybe she'd write a song about it, about strangers coming and going.

Out of sheer determination, Jennie made life return to normal. She'd tended her horse, and talked to her manager, Phil Summers, when the shrill cry of the telephone made her jump up from the piano. She tinkered with a melody and a four-bar break that just wasn't jelling. Mostly she waited.

Making a dinner she knew she wouldn't enjoy, she tried to eat, staring at the back of Jake's computer. Finally she packed the machine off to a corner on the floor and finished a meal she promptly forgot. She took a cool bath, only to get dressed again, because it was too early to go to bed.

It was almost nine when they returned. The noises were the same—thuds, voices. She saw lights in the bunkhouses, and wondered where they'd gotten the power. A group of men congregated around the trough, using the hose to rinse themselves off. Realizing that was their only shower, Jennie left them to their privacy, picking up a book she'd been in no hurry to read.

At eleven o'clock she was still awake, listening to the sounds of life across the drive. She felt a shard of guilt that she'd shown them such anger the day before. She really ought to thank them. They were there to help, after all.

Someone had brought a radio, and the men were singing along. A cool evening breeze filtered through the screen door, and Jennie was drawn out onto the long porch. She stood on the wooden planks in her bare feet and listened to the melody of deep voices, a smile crossing her face. The song was one of hers.

Jennie could almost hear her manager proclaiming, when 'Montana' had gone platinum, "Between your song and John Denver's 'Take Me Home Country Roads,' we'll have the campfire-sing-along market cornered, dammit! They'll be singing this for the next twenty years."

"Isn't that good?"

"Hell, no! You don't get royalties from Boy Scouts singing around a campfire!"

She laughed softly. "They're still singing it, Phil," she'd tell him next time he called to read her a royalty statement, as he'd done earlier in the day.

"I can read, Phil. Just mail it to me," she'd said.

He'd kept right on talking, using whatever pretext he could find to check up on her and sound her out on making a comeback. Luckily for her, he never caught her at a moment such as this. Those men didn't believe blindly in her. They didn't need her, or cling to every line she wrote. They sang for the love of it, and "Montana" was a good song.

Jennie leaned against the house in the cool darkness and hummed along, singing harmony parts usually left to backup singers. The song ended, and another of her "Greatest Hits" began.

Must be a tape player, she thought, idly analyzing the flow of the lyrics from five years' distance.

The gentle breeze fluttered past her along with the flute solo. Instead of the antiseptic studio she'd been remembering, filled with cups of cold coffee and cigarette butts, she smelled the scent of pine, a hint of smoke, and the heavy smell of dusty range grass.

She couldn't have said how she knew Jake was there. Maybe it was the subtle, almost unconscious aroma of smoke that carried his scent out of the dark. She had the uneasy, familiar feeling he was watching her. Her heartbeat accelerated like a tempo change—a little harder, a little faster.

The darkness at the end of the veranda was impenetrable. For minutes Jennie gazed into it, willing herself to be calm, wondering if she'd imagined it all. A shadow. A dream.

Jake stepped into the pale light cast by the quarter-moon. Without moving he looked Jennie up and down. He was chewing a piece of long grass. He tossed it onto the drive. In the silence that had descended around them, Jennie almost believed she heard it hit the ground.

Four

Her shoulders were bare. It was the first thing Jake noticed. She was wearing a white tank top, and her arms were pale in what little light there was. She had on a peasant skirt with a flounce that ended at her calves. It was of a filmy cotton material, moving almost imperceptibly in the soft breeze.

After dinner with the men, Jake had gone walking, wanting to wear off the strain of the day, of having fought a fire they'd put out, only to have an ember flare and the whole thing start over. He needed the quiet. Studying fires was never clean and simple. When your mind was full of thoughts of a woman who didn't want you, it got a lot more complicated.

Coming around the dark house, he'd assumed she'd gone to bed. He'd been going to tell the men to keep it down. Then the white of her blouse had caught his eye. The sound of her voice singing softly had made him stay.

She sounded happy, singing, but tenuously so. If he weren't careful he'd think of her as vulnerable right now. No telling where that would lead.

She hadn't said anything since he'd stepped onto the porch. She had barely moved.

"I was watching," he said. And listening, he added silently. "I hope you don't mind."

Jennie's heart beat faster at the sound of his voice. Her slow, deep breaths had been working to calm her, until he'd spoken. She felt lucky to be able to keep some form of control in her voice. "That's twice in two days. Getting to be a bad habit."

"A hard one to break."

She'd spoken too soon. She shouldn't have mentioned the other morning. It didn't help her heartbeat to remember his watching her while she'd been . . . sleeping.

He was within touching distance of her. He stood on one side of the front door, and she leaned against the house on the other side, for some reason unable to move.

"It's all right," she said, her voice a little louder, firmer. "It was my career, remember? I'm used to having people watch me."

"Not the way I did."

Her eyes were round and black in the dark, and focused on his. "I'm used to people who think they know me better than they do, just because they're acquainted with the surface details of my life." She sank her hands into the pockets hidden in the folds of her skirt, making it sway around her legs. That was when Jake noticed she was barefoot.

Bare feet, bare legs, bare shoulders. He wondered if the top and skirt were the only things she had on. He pictured taking them off to find out, and her letting him. He clenched his jaw and looked toward the bunkhouse.

Someone changed the tape to Alabama's "Greatest Hits." The men's voices were muffled. Either they were settling down for the night, or the poker game was getting serious.

"You look cool," Jake said quietly, stepping closer. "You smell like flowers."

"I don't wear—"

"Soap, not perfume."

"Oh. I took a bath," she said, feeling ridiculous at the sound of her own words, feeling cornered. The lapped boards of the house were at her back. She had nowhere to run, and her will to move was dissolving.

"I'm sorry if I don't smell as good. It's hard to get the smoke out of my clothes."

"Don't get so close to fires."

"Can't help it. It flared in a direction we didn't want it to go in today. Luckily we were there to divert it."

Jennie stiffened, afraid to ask if it was moving toward her ranch. "And?"

"And we ended up working instead of studying. I didn't make many notes."

"Then you won't need the computer."

"Not tonight." He moved closer, his palm flat on the wall beside her as he leaned his weight on his outstretched arm.

The acrid tang of smoke was sharp. Jennie didn't know why her heart redoubled its erratic beat. Maybe it was the idea of his being in danger, the excitement, risk, worry. Though worry shouldn't have entered into it, she realized.

Taking her hands out of her pockets she smoothed the skirt. This man obviously could take care of himself. Back safe and sound, here he was talking to her. Wasn't it someone to talk to that she'd missed so much at dinner?

She tucked a wisp of hair behind her ear where it

came loose from her braid in a nervous, self-conscious gesture. She linked her fingers in front of her. At least she looked casual. "Where did they get the lights?" She nodded toward the bunkhouse.

"Battery-powered lamps."

They listened to the crickets and the sound of far-off laughter.

"So you were a fireman today instead of a programmer."

"Uh-huh."

"What did you do?"

"Dug a lot of fire lines. We use shovels more than hoses." He chuckled softly, unaware of how Jennie twisted her fingers at the warm, inviting sound. "Hoses wouldn't do a lot of good."

Jennie thought of the horse trough and the other hose attached to the house. They wouldn't offer much protection.

"Your ranch is safe, Jennie. If it were heading toward Lone Pine, we'd call in the bombers."

"It has to pass me before it hits Lone Pine."

"Bombardiers dump fire retardant on it two thousand gallons at a time. After that the men move in and dig the fire line, put out the hot spots."

She reached up without thinking and touched his wrist, bringing his palm down to where she could see it. He said they'd been digging all day. The raw blisters on his hand showed it. She touched them gingerly, then ran her fingers down his life line. It was hard to distinguish in the darkness. Her touch told her it was long and unbroken And his love line? she wondered.

He folded his fingers over hers. She pulled away quickly, grasping her hands behind her. If he asked, she'd say she'd been curious, that was all. "So what happened to your asbestos forest?"

It took Jake a minute to forget her touch. Her hand had barely spanned his wrist. Her fingertips had been cautious and gentle.

Those times when he'd wanted her to prevent him from making a fool of himself, he'd thought her anger would keep them apart. But he forgot how delicate she could be, how vulnerable under the facade. What had closed her off, made her cloak herself in anger and demand that the world stand back? She barked, but he sensed she didn't bite. In fact, he got the feeling she'd purr if he touched her just right—or claw. He found both ideas too appealing.

He cleared his throat with a low rumble. "Asbestos? It did its job. It kept the fire from moving in a straight line. Then the wind carried the embers over it and we ended up fighting flare-ups. That was all."

Some *all*, he thought. The unpredictable swirl of wind in the mountain valley had started and helped spread three fires in the course of four hours, jumping the forest that should have contained it. It could be days before they had it out for good. "The main thing is to keep it from moving down Owens Valley if the wind picks up."

"Can't have that." If Jennie sounded untroubled it was because her mind was elsewhere. She was more interested in Jake Kramer than where the fire was moving. "Is it exciting, fighting fires, Jake?"

"Can be." He wasn't sure he believed it even as he was saying it. Looking at her he could think of a hundred more exciting things. Such as hearing her say his name again. "I was kind of distracted today."

"Why?" she asked casually, to keep the conversation moving.

He'd been thinking of her, wanting her, and all the words he could think of to explain it only made the situation worse. So without thinking, he touched the inside of her elbow. It was soft and slightly moist. Tendrils of hair clung to her neck, still damp from her bath. He wiped the hair away with his fingers.

Jennie shuddered, and hoped it didn't show. "Don't."

He stroked her cheek. She turned away, but tilted her head toward his touch. She'd sent him away before, Jake remembered, resisted him. He'd walked away once. He didn't want a woman who didn't want him. He had to know where he stood.

At every break in the fire he'd thought of her. He thought of her arguing, and got angry. He thought of their conversation over dinner, and smiled. He thought of touching her, of kissing her, and his gut tightened and he felt the heat growing in his blood.

"Jennie . . ." His hand light on her neck, he pulled her toward him, wanting to kiss her again.

"Jake, I don't want this."

"You think I do? I've played it safe for as long as I care to. Pretending I don't want you lasted a day. Your acting as if you don't want me worked a little longer."

"And if I mean it?" She didn't know how the breathiness got into her voice.

"Risk it, Jennie. See where this leads."

"But you'll only be here a few days."

"And you've been here two years." It was one of the few things about her he knew for a fact. The rest he was learning as he went. "Let me show you what you've missed."

His mouth didn't claim hers; it asked her for permission. His closed lips just met hers, and he felt the last of her resistance trembling there.

"Jennie," he whispered, "let me in."

The sounds of the bunkhouse faded against the

pounding in her ears. The grass wavered like her resolve. The whirring insects of the night hummed in her blood. The glittering stars were like a thousand sparks in her veins, warning flares. She'd never been neutral toward him. They'd started out being intimate and had been fighting it ever since.

Her tongue darted out to wet her lips and met his. His mouth opened to accept it, and she was lost.

He took his time wrapping her in his arms, until she felt the press of his body and the stunning, complete surrender of her own. Curving into his hardness, her hands explored the bulge of his muscular arms, the breadth of his shoulders, the angular blades of his back, and the soft, straw-blond hair she could almost hear rustling through her fingers.

His moan was caught in her mouth as he pulled her to him. Every time she moved against him he felt the flames of desire grow hotter. The night breeze had become a Santa Ana blowing across the high mountains. He could feel her skin through the thin cotton of her top, feel her skirt swaying around his legs. More than anything else, he felt her mouth, hot, open, entreating. She took his tongue, sucking and teasing, driving him into an abyss of building need. Moans and half-whispered names were lost between them.

Her body arched into the sweet ache she'd aroused in him, her hips meeting the growing rhythm of his sex, where he prodded the parting of her thighs in a potent, repetitive move, a fiery hint of what they could share together.

A shout from the bunkhouse reached them, laughter, loud music. The insects resumed their chant, sounding to her like crowd noise and static.

Jake set her down slowly as her arms slid from around his neck, her toes touching the boards of the porch. She realized for the first time he'd lifted her off it. Her legs came together from where they'd clutched either side of his thighs.

She didn't want to stop, but thoughts crowded in, consequences. Once, long ago in her past, she'd needed in the same way. He'd been a faceless stranger, a man she'd met backstage. Then she had known what her young friend Karen had been searching for so desperately, to be held, to be pleasured with no befores and no afters, no hopes or fears or wants confusing everything—just bodies and need. And the morning after that one desperate encounter, she'd known how empty Karen had felt. How used. How disappointed. How ashamed.

It disturbed her that she wanted Jake in the same reckless way. And it deeply frightened her that their union, no matter how brief, would never be as superficial. Of that she was certain.

"Can we go into the bedroom?" He tilted his head toward the room off the veranda, where he'd first seen her. She took his hand and led him there. He tried to see, but it was impossible. All he felt was her touch, magnified a thousand times in the dark. "Jennie." He put her arms around his waist. His voice was tight. "I'll take it slow. I don't want to hurt you."

"Make love to me, Jake. Now. Make it fast." Maybe if she didn't think, if she denied all the feelings he was awakening, maybe then she could have the love without the pain. If so, pain would be the only emotion she avoided. All the others were simmering dangerously close to the surface, one touch away from overflowing.

Her hands clutching his back, her nails digging in in an agony of desire, she barely heard his panted words of love. "Lord, Jennie, do you know what you're doing to me?" She laughed softly. He could have exploded right there. "I've been crazy for you since I first saw you. You're in my blood."

"Now," she pleaded. If only he'd hurry so she could make herself believe it was only a physical, basic need, just a man and a woman. It could be satiated.

"I need a woman like you, Jennie. Your strength, your fire. A woman who isn't afraid to say what she wants. I wanted you to be here when I got back."

"Don't lie to me, Jake, please."

"I'm not. All day I wanted to talk to you. It scared me how much I needed to."

She broke away from him with a sudden, surprising twist and fled onto the veranda. "You don't need me," she cried. "Don't say that! I'm not your savior. I can't help anyone but myself."

His first reaction was to lash out in return. "And you were going to help yourself to me?"

"Yes," she said. "Don't act like it's more than it is."

She couldn't have stunned him more if she'd slapped him. He took a step behind her. "What am I supposed to say?" He touched her back, and she arched like a cat. "I could lie and say it's only lust. Believe me, I'm tempted, if that's what it takes." He ran a finger down her spine, and she choked back a moan. But he knew it was useless to pretend. He meant every word he'd said. "I don't know if I can keep our relationship on those terms, Jennie."

Her head was bowed, silvery blue moonlight streaking hair he wanted to touch but couldn't.

"Then go." Her voice was harder than she felt, her words final.

His touch lingered long after the sound of his boots on the wooden stairs had died out, long after his silhouette was outlined in the opening and closing bunkhouse door and she was alone again.

She hadn't wanted to hurt him. But she couldn't be needed—not again. It had been her whole life once. People grasping at her, taking pieces of her, bit by bit. She'd given and given until there wasn't anything left. Not even enough for the one person who'd needed her most. Jennie had failed her. And Karen had died. Never again would she let someone need her that badly.

The sun was up. The sky was blue, flat, and uninterrupted, stretched over the valley like a taut canvas. The day was dry and hot. Nothing has changed, Jennie said to herself as she clattered the breakfast dishes onto the table and tried to believe her own words. One day was so much like the next. But the nights . . .

"Do you mind if I get in some work?" Jake's voice startled her, and she dropped a fork.

Bending to retrieve it, Jennie tried to think. He was going to stay on his side of the fence, and she on hers. Wasn't that the conclusion they'd come to the night before?

Jake was eyeing the computer on the floor. "I figured I'd squeeze in an hour before we head out." His voice was as flat as the blue sky, and as indifferent.

Fine, if you can keep it that way, Jennie thought. "Go ahead."

Jake set up while Jennie broke eggs for an omelet she didn't feel like eating. Hoping he was too busy to notice, she scraped bits of broken eggshell out of the bowl. She dragged over the cutting board and chopped green pepper and onion, biting her tongue when her mind wandered and she nicked her finger.

The memory of the previous night was embarrassing, mortifying, and he was making her nervous.

Even with her back turned, she sensed every move he made. From the strength of his arms lifting the machine, to his large hands punching out numbers on the keyboard. She'd felt those hands last night. She felt them now. How was she going to sit and eat with him there? She added three eggs to the skillet.

She tried to remember every scurrilous rumor invented about her in Lone Pine, the ones Karen delighted in bringing home. After the previous night, Jake Kramer probably believed every one of them. "Here."

He stopped, surprised at the plate she set in front of him. "You go ahead, I don't mind."

"I've got another one cooking."

He finally looked at her instead of at the plate. "Thank you."

She watched her own omelet cook and bubble so she could spend less time sitting at the table trying not to look at him. It had been so much easier in the dark. How could she explain her actions? *I'm sorry I threw myself at you last night? That's not the real me?*

She hadn't meant to be so blatant. Loneliness wasn't a pretty emotion. Two years alone had left empty places anyone would want filled and he'd found hers.

Jake worked and kept the distance to which they'd silently agreed. Fingers linked tightly under his chin, he stared at the screen. He pecked harshly at the keys. He sipped the coffee she'd set in front of him, wondering why the hell he was there. She'd been careful not to get too close when setting down the cup, he noticed, yet her scent lingered.

He pulled a sheaf of wrinkled notepaper out of his pocket. One page was burned in half. "Notes from the fire," he replied to her astonished, unasked question.

"Mmm," she said, stirring sugar into her coffee. It wasn't smart to be caught looking interested. "Seems I always smell smoke when you're around."

"So do I," he said, and their gazes locked.

Heat rising to her face, Jennie turned to scrape the omelet onto her plate.

Jake looked at his screen. He slapped down a curling piece of notepaper with the flat of his hand.

Since her place at the table had already been set, she edged onto a chair catercorner to him and concentrated on her food. She didn't mean to watch his mouth pursed in contemplation, or the slope of his cheek over his jaw, the taut shaved skin she suddenly remembered as if she'd rubbed her cheek against it minutes before. How could she have forgotten that? Or the feel of his hair between her fingers?

He stretched his legs under the table and bumped her knee. Jennie jumped, but covered her mistake quickly by clearing dishes. She couldn't think with him there, and she needed to. A good talking to herself on what lonely, desperate women were capable of might set her straight. If that was what she was, it was better to face it now. "I'm going out."

Jake raised a brow. "There aren't many places to go out to on a mountain."

"To the stable," she said, annoyed at having to explain herself to him and at the fact that he'd even care. Her emotions were too close to the surface, irritated and raw.

Jake listened to the slam of the screen door. She wasn't happy. Neither was he. But he'd honor her distance. She had her terms—not to be needed. He had his. In Jake's experience, life stayed simple as long as a woman knew what she wanted. His ex-wife had taught him the lesson more than once. Anything was better than having a woman walk out on you simply because she'd changed her mind.

Jennie sat in the corner of the stable, wanting to pace, wanting some action. She felt surrounded, her solitude invaded by men. She forced herself to sit as still as possible on the bench. Tapping her boot, she watched Chick work.

"Hope you don't mind," the older man said.

Jennie picked a piece of straw out of a bale and chewed. "How can I?" She quickly amended the rude remark and felt the tight line of her mouth relax into a smile. "Looks like you're doing a fine job." The man obviously had Glaze's best interest at heart.

"Always been fond of horses." The brush fit snugly in Chick's hand, the gleam in the horse's coat coming through with each stroke.

"Mmm." Jennie gave in to the urge to pace, but her movements set off Glaze. He wanted to get moving too. Damn, she thought, sitting on the bench again, now she was making the horse nervous.

But when she stopped moving she started thinking. Thoughts of the previous night would sneak up on her, making her edgy, unsure. It wasn't easy to admit how far she would have gone with Jake. Standing at the porch rail waiting for him to go, her body had ached for him to stay. Hours later in the dark, she could still feel his hands and the thrumming response they'd created inside her. She'd returned his feelings in full. She'd opened to him as a parched flower did to water. Their mouths had suckled and sought and found what they needed. Knowing it would be temporary, knowing he'd be gone when the fire had burned out, she would have taken him into her bed.

If only he hadn't said he needed her. If only he'd lied and said he *wanted* her. It would have been so simple. And she would have been so willing. And when it was over?

She almost blushed, thinking about it. But he hadn't lied. At least he's honest, she thought wryly.

She sighed, her mouth dry, beads of sweat already forming. It was eight A.M. Seeing that Chick had matters so completely in hand, her only option was conversation. "So you know horses."

"Know 'em pretty well. I was a cowboy as a teenager."

Jennie watched Chick and Glaze go through the grooming routine as if they'd been together for years. The horse pranced sideways, and Chick settled him down with a few murmured words.

"And Jake," she asked, "you know him pretty well?"

Walking around to the far side of the horse, Chick allowed himself a smile.

She heard him chuckle as if he'd known her question was coming. Darn it, she had a right to ask questions. "I don't really mind you men living out here, but I don't know if I feel secure with him in my house."

"I can't say how secure you might be, Ms. Cisco."

Jennie missed the hint of sarcasm completely. Having faced her dilemma head on, she was up and pacing, flicking her braid agitatedly over her shoulder. "A total stranger has just moved into my kitchen. Day and night he's working on that thing." She was exaggerating again. Somehow, where Jake was concerned she blew everything out of proportion.

Chick waited for her to simmer down, choosing his words carefully. "I don't know what to tell you. Jake's a decent man. Too decent, sometimes. Even so, I'd trust him with my life. As for his being in your house, I suppose you could expect to be about as safe as any man and woman can be."

That was little consolation to Jennie.

"I've known Jake since he was a teenager. We worked a couple ranches together."

"He was a cowboy?"

"For a while, until he met up with fire fighting. Jake knows his business. When it comes to taking risks he can be pretty hardheaded, but he's never foolhardy. I'd say you're fortunate to have him looking after you."

"Hmmph."

"And your ranch," Chick was careful to add.

"What about my ranch? Is it safe?"

"Fires are about as unpredictable as the wind. And I mean that to the letter."

"Jake said—" She paused. Here she was, quoting Jake Kramer.

"What did he say?"

Jennie toyed with a bridle and a blanket.

"Too hot to ride today," Chick said, killing her escape route.

She smiled in spite of her mood. He really did have the best interest of the horse at heart. "Jake said the main priority was to keep the fire from moving too close to Lone Pine or down toward Keeler."

"He didn't make you any promises about this place?"

"No."

"Then he told you honestly. It isn't like Jake to promise something he can't back up. No one man can stop a fire."

She put her hands on her hips and confronted Chick as he finished with the horse. "Will you help me put Glaze in the trailer, Chick? There's a stable closer to Owens Lake where I'll board him until this is over." It was the safest place for Glaze just then, although Jennie felt she was losing her last and only friend. She was hemmed in by people: in her house, her stables, her bunkhouses. Voices, radios, and trucks. She needed to get away. Ironically, town was suddenly a refuge she sought instead of a personal appearance she avoided.

At the sound of the pickup pulling the trailer out from behind the stable, Jake raced out of the house. "Where are you going?" he demanded, his hand clamped on the driver's door.

Jennie was so startled, she didn't answer. It had been a long time since someone had questioned her comings and goings. Her temper was on a short leash, and it was no time to challenge her. Her blood boiling, her voice was the coldest thing on the mountain. "I'm taking Glaze to town."

"I want to check on how the fire's moved since last night."

He was being reasonable. He was probably right. She wasn't hearing a word. Maybe it was the heat, maybe the fire. Maybe it was him and her.

"Go ahead," she said. "What you do doesn't concern me, as long as you keep my ranch safe. I'm taking Glaze to board." She let the clutch out slowly, and the pickup started to move.

Jake walked along beside it. "A stable's a good idea. I wouldn't want a panicky horse to deal with on top of everything else. While you're at it, why not pack a bag and stay down there yourself?"

Jennie's look could have set a batch of tinder ablaze.

Though he didn't like seeing her fierce look, he had to admit he was relieved. There'd be no better way to keep his distance than to have her evacuate voluntarily. Then maybe he could concentrate on his fire instead of on how she tasted when he kissed her, how her skin felt when she shivered because of a dry breeze on a hot night.

He heard Joe on the radio, checking weather conditions. "Just wait until we track the fire. The wind's changed since last night."

Jennie pressed her boot slowly on the gas pedal. "Glaze doesn't like being trailered, and I don't like reporting my comings and goings."

"Just tell me which road you're taking. Dammit, Jennie, I need to know."

There was that word again, *need*. She put the pedal down.

He was damned if he was going to run after her, he thought, hitting the door with the side of his fist. He shouted a curse as she turned the truck out onto the road, the trailer following meekly behind.

Five

Harbring's was a stable with a solid reputation. Glaze had been boarded there two years before, when Jennie had had to rush to Los Angeles. He'd done all right. He'd do all right this time, she told herself. When the fire was out and everyone was gone, they'd go back to their lives. Jennie promised him that as she headed into town.

Town was as usual. The locals in the grocery store recognized her and didn't look twice as she filled her cart with food. A closer look would have told them steaks and beer were unusual purchases for her. She considered baked beans a perfect picnic touch, but with the canned food her fire fighters had brought they'd probably had enough beans.

Her fire fighters? She shrugged inwardly. After all, she wasn't so stubborn that she wouldn't give them credit for protecting her ranch. The least she could do was feed them a decent meal, she decided. They'd been friendly, not too boisterous. She remembered the music wafting up from the bunk-houses and immediately squelched any memories associated with the previous night.

Was her embarrassment any justification for treating Jake so rudely? No. Should she apologize? Yes. Would she? Only if this store sold five-pound bags of nerve. Something about that man made her want to run in the other direction. It wasn't a pleasant sensation.

As she wandered down the aisles, the only part of the night before she could recall without blushing was the old songs. She didn't listen to the radio much. She worked on her own music, writing songs she never performed, sending them to a manager who hadn't stopped pleading for her to make a comeback. He sold them to other singers, and she did well enough to keep her in groceries and allow her to pay property taxes on her ranch.

She hoped the fans had forgotten her. She'd instructed Phil Summers to stop forwarding their letters. She didn't want to mislead them or carry around the guilt for letting them down. She was out of the rat race, and out she'd stay.

She stacked food on the check-out counter and watched it being tallied and packed into brown paper sacks.

"You're Jennie Cisco, aren't you?"

It was the sure way the woman had made the statement that made Jennie feel immediately trapped between her cart and the woman behind her in the narrow check-out lane.

"I'm Eileen Wesson. You've heard about the fire, of course."

With twelve men camped in her front yard, how could she not? "Yes, I have," she said to the stylishly dressed woman behind her. Jennie tried a wan smile, failed, and left it at that.

Eileen wasn't finished. "Did you hear about the Marlows?"

Jennie shook her head and watched the cashier's fingers tapping up the total on the register.

"Their ranch burned out Tuesday. House, everything. It moved so fast, they were lucky to get themselves out."

Jennie felt deeply sorry for the family. She could imagine losing a home. It had taken her so long to find hers.

Eileen Wesson was waiting for a reply.

"I'm sorry to hear that," Jennie put in.

"It's settled in again, so I've heard. The fire."

Jennie wrote out her check and was waiting for it to be approved, when she felt a hand on her arm. Why did people feel they had the right to grab at her? she wondered. She took a deep breath to calm the flutters in her stomach. She knew memories of being pawed at by out-of-control crowds were coloring her perceptions.

She took another breath and looked up. The woman was patting her frosted hair and smiling. She'd caught the flash of fury in Jennie's eyes and had removed her hand.

"The reason I'm so glad I bumped into you is that we're having a benefit—a dinner at the high school, with canned goods and clothes and anything anyone can contribute."

Jennie glanced at her cart laden with food and sighed in relief. This was something she could willingly give. "I'd be happy to donate. How much do you need?"

"Oh, not from you! You have so much more to give. We were wondering if you'd sing."

Jennie looked over Eileen's shoulder for the mysterious *we*. "Really," she said dryly, knowing the whole thing was out of the question.

She also realized, with a sinking feeling, that it

would take more than a simple, "No, thanks" to get her out of the situation. Eileen Wesson looked like the persistent type, enthusiastic and unfailingly polite. Just the kind of woman to get things done in a small town.

"There's a little stage at the high school, but we hoped you'd come. We'd raise a lot more money that way. A drawing card, you know? I hope it doesn't sound crass, but people are in need." Eileen smiled and touched her hair again.

So why did the mere thought of performing make Jennie's heart beat like a drum synthesizer on "fast"? When had all the air in the store gone stale? For a panicky moment she considered referring everything to her manager. Let Phil put the woman off.

Jennie stuck with the truth. "I'm sorry. I don't perform anymore."

"Well, we all know you don't. But this would only be for the local crowd. In a school gym. I mean, really, is that performing?"

"I'm sorry, I can't." Jennie felt the blood rushing to her cheeks. Why couldn't the check-out girl go faster? Surely she didn't need Jennie's ID to accept the check.

"It's for a family with three children and no house. And no clothes other than what they were wearing."

"I'd be happy to give them some food." Or any amount of money, she thought. Phil had always said she was a soft touch. In years past she'd done as many free shows as paid, if someone convinced her she was needed. There it was: Need, again, along with its companions, Responsibility and Guilt.

Obviously Eileen Wesson wasn't used to being turned down. Her social polish was slipping, her voice strained inside a stretched smile. "You have a gift, something you can give that not many people could. Wouldn't it be worth it for people in need? Like 'We Are The World,' or something?"

Jennie wanted to scream. Didn't people realize singing and stardom weren't answers to the world's problems? A former celebrity dropping in at a school gym wasn't going to rebuild anybody's home. The glass walls were closing in on her.

"I don't perform," Jennie said abruptly, pushing her cart blindly toward the exit. "I'm sorry." She almost ran through the parking lot. All right, so the townspeople would go on thinking she was a cold-hearted bitch. "If I can't help me, how can I help you?" she said to nobody, shoving the grocery bags into the pickup.

She slammed the door, the thud reminding her of Jake's fist this morning. She pungently repeated his curse.

She'd always seen herself as determined. She couldn't have gotten far in her profession without a good deal of backbone. Her first album had been called "Face the Music," and she had done that, blatantly working out her insecurities in her songs. She'd earned a reputation for unflinching honesty and razor-fine sensitivity, a reputation she'd believed in. Hightailing it to the hills didn't sit well with that image.

She swore again as she ground the gears and down-shifted, heading southeast, straight into the mountains. When running from fears didn't work, sometimes facing them head on did. Jake Kramer was one fear. All day she'd been hiding from her reaction to him. She had to discover what her feelings for him really were. Her absolute refusal to be drawn back into performing was another fear that needed analyzing. Then there was the fear of being needed—and of failing. For an insightful person she'd conveniently avoided a lot of tough questions lately.

There was also the small matter of a raging brush fire threatening everything she owned.

Where was the fire now? How fast was it moving? When would it reach her ranch? Could they stop it?

"Fear Number One, here I come. I'm going to get the lay of this land myself."

The pickup climbed the mountain road. Jennie wheeled around a corner so tightly, two bags of groceries fell over. She elbowed them back into place. Lacking a radio, she was haunted by an instant replay of the scene in the store. The earnest pleading in Eileen's voice, her none-too-subtle application of guilt, Jennie's cowardly reaction. All of it grated on her nerves. Her mind searched in vain for a kinder refusal, her conscience paying her in spades for turning tail instead. Midday heat built up like tension in the cab of the truck. The end result—she was itching for a fight.

Both Jake and Eileen expected her to give and give to satisfy their needs. And would it make any difference if she did? People had to stand on their own two feet. She couldn't help them. No matter how she tried or what she did, they couldn't expect her to save them.

Tears blinded her eyes. Downshifting too late on a steep incline, the truck stalled and jolted to a stop. One bag of groceries tipped forward, spilling over on the floor mat. "Now you've done it, idiot." But the harsh words didn't stop the tears.

Karen. Jennie had tried so hard, convinced that with love and understanding, she could help the girl. She'd offered support when Karen needed it, independence when she believed the troubled fifteen-year-old was on firmer emotional ground. Nothing had worked. Then Karen had run away.

"She spent her life running away," Jennie said,

quietly sounding it out in the cab of the truck. "From home and her parents, from loneliness with sex, from reality with drugs. From me, because I tried to help." She drove slowly, thinking, wondering why thoughts of Karen still haunted her and if she'd ever find an answer.

Turning a sharp corner, a blanket of smoke was visible in the distance, clinging to the mountainside, tips of pines poking through it. It brought Jennie's attention back to the present. There were more immediate problems to face. She'd have to be careful driving through the area.

The smoke disappeared behind a curve as the truck climbed higher into the mountains. The road backtracked, always going up. The pickup's tires spit out loose gravel and dust. The forest crept to the road's edge, towering pines and dry brush. The bushes were covered with light dust—gray leaves, gray bushes, smothered and dead.

Around the next curve the tang of smoke nipped the air again. Jennie wrinkled her nose, blinked, and kept driving. One more curve and she'd see the entire side of the mountain and gauge for herself the extent of the blaze.

Then it hit her full on—a wall of smoke as dense as fog, rolling over the road through the trees, escaping down a steep grade on the other side.

Jennie gasped and choked. Hurrying to roll up her windows, she hit her elbow on the horn, the noise startling her, her coughs interspersed with curses.

She threw the pickup into reverse, whipping backward into a curve. Then forward, then back, trying to turn around on the narrow road. She didn't realize the rear tire had slipped off the hard-pack onto a sandy shoulder until she threw the pickup into first and gunned it.

The tire spun, digging into the sand. Covering a sinking feeling with more curses, she put the clutch in and slowly let it out, giving the engine as little gas as possible. The truck rocked forward and stopped, accompanied by the high whine of spinning tires.

Jennie wiped her eyes hastily with the back of her hand. Her heart pounded like the throb of the engine. She knew it would help if she could get out of the truck and throw some pine branches under the rear tire. Any traction would help.

She looked out at the smoke; it would be insane to get out of the truck now. A curtain of gray was spreading down the road the way she'd come, surrounding her. She had to move.

She put the truck in reverse, rocked it, put it in first, rocked it. Sand and gravel flew off the back tire and shotgunned against the empty pickup bed. With each attempt she was digging herself in deeper. Soon a trench had been dug in the soft shoulder and the tires threw up nothing but hissing sand.

The cab was a furnace, with the windows rolled tight. Smoke crawled in anyway, acrid and searing. Jennie yanked up her shirt, undid the bottom buttons, and covered her mouth and nose, hastily wiping away tears and sweat. Flooring the gas pedal and laying on the horn in sheer frustration, she listened to the engine's angry, empty roar and silently cursed her own stupidity.

There was only one way out. Could she pull down a handful of pine branches before being overcome by the smoke? Would the traction work? Was she panicking? Could anything be more dangerous than sitting there waiting to pass out? Telling herself she should have acted when the idea had first come to her was no comfort. She took as deep a breath as she could manage and reached for the door handle.

It was gone. Open. Rough hands were grasping her and dragging her out.

"What are you doing here?" he shouted. Even with a bandanna covering half his face, she recognized Jake Kramer.

Her eyes were watering, and the thin cloth of her shirt wasn't keeping out much smoke. She could just make out the yellow Jeep parked in the swirling haze as he lifted her into it and they took off down the road. How he could see, she didn't dare guess. A curtain of dust and smoke hung over the road. It cleared suddenly as they rounded a bend and lurched to a halt.

In the angry seconds that followed, parts of Jake's lecture registered. She'd been crazy, taken a stupid risk. What could she have been thinking?

The fact that she had had the same fleeting thoughts while trapped in her truck didn't mean she wanted to hear them from him. Before she'd even had a chance to feel gratitude he was giving her a lesson in humiliation. Some rescuer. Worse yet, every time she tried a snappy comeback she was overcome with coughing.

Out of the corner of her eye she glimpsed his pained expression. He winced every time she choked on an angry retort. Overcome again, furious at her own weakness, Jennie bent over double from a vicious round of coughing, her arms wrapped tightly around her waist. When she glanced at Jake his jaw was tense, his eyes set on the horizon, hands clutching the wheel. She'd get no sympathy from him.

His fist clenched, he punched the button on the CB. "Burt, this is Radio One."

"Come in, Number-One Son."

The playful reply wasn't lost on Jake. It meant things were under relative control a mile back. "You were right about the noise," he said, "it was a truck stuck on the shoulder."

"Civilians?"

"Our very own, Jennie Cisco. She panicked and tried to back up. Dug herself in."

Jennie took a breath to argue and choked instead.

Jake looked away, pressing the button tighter. "I'm taking her down. How's it look your way?"

"Exciting, but nothing we can't handle. See you at dinner."

"Right."

Jake drove fast, swerving down mountain roads, accelerating up passes. The wind in the open Jeep pelted Jennie, but she didn't mind. Through the smoke that permeated her lungs, she could tell it was clean mountain air, pure oxygen. The only problem was keeping it in.

She wiped her watery eyes with the hem of her shirt. Because the catch in her throat threatened her with a cough every time she opened her mouth, it was a few minutes before she dared talk. "All right, maybe I shouldn't have gone up there." It was weak, but it was a start. She owed him a debt of thanks and an apology for this morning. She was getting to it.

Jake said nothing. A pulse beating on the side of his jaw was the only indication he was listening.

"I wanted to see where the fire was going. It's my ranch, my home! I have some right to know what's going on."

"You could have asked me." His voice was sharp and sarcastic, his gaze on the road. He manhandled the steering wheel around an unusually tight corner, and Jennie clung to the dash. When they hit a straightaway she buckled her seat belt. The road fell away sharply on her side. There were no guardrails.

In her enclosed pickup she never minded. In an open Jeep, with Jake driving, it made her nervous— and angry. He wasn't giving her a chance, judging her without waiting for an explanation.

"So I made a mistake! Say 'I told you so' and be done with it!"

"Civilians should know better than to blunder into a fire zone. Couldn't you see the smoke?"

"Not until I came around the curve. Then I hit it so fast—" A hacking cough shook her, and she couldn't go on.

Jake slowed and pulled over to the side. He watched her guardedly, one arm thrown over the back of the seat as if ready to comfort her. But something told Jake to hold back where touching Jennie Cisco was concerned, and this time he listened. If he'd listened to that voice before, his gut wouldn't be twisted the way it was, listening to her dragging in each breath.

She didn't want him. He ought to have known that by now. Whatever reason she'd used for letting him kiss her was hers alone. He hadn't been let in on it. All she said was, 'Don't need me,' and he'd ignored it and gone right on needing. He was too far gone to make rational decisions anymore. It was up to her to keep the distance between them. Fortunately for them both, she was intent on doing so.

Finally she quieted and looked over the mountains, distant valleys, and jagged peaks. Everything was clear and sharp, as if she were seeing it for the first time. "I tried to back up," she said to the empty air falling away down the mountainside. "I was getting out of there as fast as I could."

"You were stuck." Jake rammed the Jeep into gear and took off. "You panicked."

"I didn't."

"You panicked." The roar of the engine being forced

into third stopped that argument. Jennie found another.

"Where are we going?"

"The back way."

"If you think you're going to take me to town for safekeeping, don't bother. I'll get a ride from somebody and be back at the ranch before dark. You might force your way onto my land, but you're not kicking me off my ranch."

Jake laughed humorlessly. "You have no idea what my *force* is like, honey."

She knew it was an idle threat, but he was big enough to make her think twice. By then the chance for a fast comeback was gone. The fight in her wasn't. If he thought he was going to evacuate her from the ranch by driving her to town, he was in for the argument of his life.

They drove on, both as jumpy and mad as if the seats were made of cactus needles. Then Jennie recognized the approaching hills and knew they were heading for her ranch. It was a small victory, one she was intent on savoring. "Home sweet home," she said sarcastically.

Jake slammed on the brakes in the drive, causing a cloud of dust to rise up and overtake them.

Jennie unfastened her seat belt and hopped out fast. If he thought he was going to dump her and drive off, she had other ideas. Leaving him in the dust that morning hadn't been the nicest thing to do, but it was a good deal kinder than anything that occurred to her just then.

So she took her sweet time walking around the front of the Jeep, pausing to lean on the hood and wipe some dust off her boots. The man had saved her life, and immediately treated her so rudely, she'd had no chance to thank him. If she couldn't make him pay, she'd make him wait.

Jake gunned the engine, eager to be gone before her irritating behavior made him any angrier. Didn't she realize she could have been killed? He shut the ignition off with a twist of his wrist and let the clutch out so fast, the car jerked forward. Jennie jumped, and gave him a withering stare.

In four quick strides he had her by the shoulders. "You think I won't evacuate you to town the minute it's necessary?"

"*El Dobro* is mine. I'm staying."

"If the fire comes this way, you're out!"

Jennie knew better than to struggle in his iron grip. She merely lifted her chin. "No way."

"That's my final word, Jennie."

"Tough. Let me go!"

Jake held her more tightly, but at arm's length. "Dammit, you almost got killed! You were minutes away from being overcome by smoke. *Minutes.*"

She wrestled in his grasp, unable to think rationally.

"If I hadn't been there, if Burt hadn't heard the horn . . ."

She didn't hear the fear in his voice as she shook loose. "So what are you doing here now? Deserting your men to baby-sit me? I don't want you here!" The words were as ugly and hurting as she could make them. His touch, his nearness, were too tempting. She wanted to cling to those rescuing arms, and she wanted to run.

She could tell by the darkness in his eyes she'd pushed him too far. When he grabbed her arm it was with a tug that brought her up on her toes.

"Never accuse me of deserting my men. They've got things under control. If they didn't, Miss Prima Donna, I'd have sent someone else to baby-sit you."

Too angry to speak, she tried to walk away before the cough that had been clawing at her throat won out. She didn't get far. Doubling over, she collapsed against the Jeep, covering her mouth with both hands and coughing until she thought her lungs would tear. Jake's boots stopped inches away.

"Go away," she gasped out. "If I didn't have to scream to make myself heard around here this wouldn't have happened." She waved at him weakly. He didn't move. She stumbled toward the house, but he had other ideas.

Sweeping her roughly off her feet, he carried her toward the bunkhouse. His voice was low, his words blunt. "We're going in here."

She fought him every step of the way, writhing and kicking and coughing. But his arms were as unrelenting as iron, his face hard and expressionless. With one swift kick of his boot the door burst open, and he strode past the row of bunks to his private room. With a thump, he deposited her on his cot and left without a word, shutting the door behind him.

Jennie sat up warily, her eyes stinging, her throat raw, her breath coming shallow and fast. She had to get out of there. He was angry. Neither one of them was thinking clearly. She could still feel the granite hardness of his chest as she'd struck out at him, the effortless way he'd carried her. If force was what he really had in mind, how would she ever fight him off?

The little she knew of Jake told her he wasn't prone to using force, but it was small consolation to her now.

She followed the sound of the pounding of his boots to the far end of the bunkhouse, then lunged for the door. It was a mistake. Another fit of coughing drowned out everything, and she collapsed against the wall, shoulders heaving. When she looked up, he was standing in the doorway, an oxygen tank at his feet. He twisted the knob until air hissed out. With one hand on the back of her neck, he held the mask to her face and ordered her to breathe.

She didn't need to be told. Her lungs felt shredded, and only too happy to inhale the sweet oxygen. So pure, it was going straight to her head. Drawing in too greedily, she fought down another cough. Automatically her hand reached for the mask, and covered Jake's.

It was so small against his. It trembled. He sat her on the bed, one arm supporting her shoulders as she sagged against him.

It was stuffy in the small room. Chinks in the lathing of the old wooden walls let in light and heat. After a few minutes Jennie could breathe without the mask. She wiped the perspiration off her forehead with the back of her hand. The aroma of smoke clung to her skin. The smell brought back the sensation of suffocating in the cab of her truck. Trapped. Like a dream where you run and can't get anywhere, only it had been real. With a sudden yearning, she wished she could talk to Jake about it, but that was impossible now. They'd both said too many hurtful things. The only difference was, she hadn't meant half of hers. She shuddered and closed her eyes tightly.

Dying alone terrified her. Surrounded by emptiness with no one to care. The memory of Karen in a barren room in L.A. came back to her full force. Closed eyes couldn't shut it out. She swayed, and Jake held her steady. Minutes, he'd said, minutes away from passing out—and then dying.

She took more oxygen. Rivulets of sweat trickling inside her shirt made her shiver, although she knew it had to be a hundred degrees in the airless room.

Jake was too close, it was too hot, and she was too vulnerable. She wanted to wrap her arms around his neck and just cry. He'd probably push her away, and she couldn't take that at the moment. She concentrated on her surroundings instead, on wooden planks that formed a wall, on the worn duffel bag on the floor, clothes spilling out of it. Jake's clothes.

He felt every trembling breath she took, with the oxygen and without. He felt her leg next to his on the sagging cot, and when she began to let go of the anger and fear, he felt the tension leaving her.

When he saw the tears running down her cheeks he thought he recognized the need in her eyes. He told himself it could be for any man; it was called gratitude. He held her close and let her cry, not that it meant anything. When the storm had passed he touched her tentatively, tenderly, wiping tears away.

She touched his face in return, her lips pressing lightly to his in a thank you so sweet, he ached. Her lips parted, let him in. A gift.

"You don't have to, Jennie." His voice was as hoarse as hers, but for different reasons.

"What if I want to?" Her hand worked up his back, over the delineation of each hard muscle, then rested on the warm skin of his neck, urging his mouth to hers.

When her tongue skimmed his lips, he shuddered, and his breath was uneven. She was alive, and Jennie wanted that more than anything. Death had come too close. It would have been pointless, meaningless, and she would have been alone. She wanted to pull back from the edge, to seize life, to face everything she feared most. And that meant facing this man and what he was beginning to mean to her. Their tongues met, and she gave a small moan. She wanted to feel physically, emotionally, utterly alive, and Jake Kramer was the man to make her feel that way.

The sound of her shallow breaths mingled with his low, increasingly ragged ones. His palm eased the fabric of her shirt against her skin as his hands moved up and down her body. She seemed fragile now, not the fierce, demanding woman who'd wanted everything on her terms the night before. He could almost span her ribs with his hands, and, as they came around, his thumbs grazed the sides of her breasts, and she shivered.

Her breath on his cheek, the way her hands curled through his hair and urged him nearer—everything coaxed him into continuing something he'd sworn to avoid. The catch in her throat when she gasped as he ran his fingers boldly over her breasts made it impossible for him to push her away. "Jennie . . ."

She touched her lips lightly to his cheek, smelling the smoke that couldn't threaten her anymore. "Let me touch you." She didn't wait for an answer. Unbuttoning his shirt, her fingers fanned out on his skin—hot, slick skin. She teased him with her fingertips.

Just her *touching* him made him want to drag her onto the cot and feel her body beneath his. "I'm only a man, babe. I can't take much more of this."

"You wanted more last night." Her fingers curled through the hair on his chest, over the tight peaks of his nipples.

"You didn't want me then."

She looked up at him, drawn not only by the tension in his body but by the hunger in his eyes. And yet he was withholding a part of himself, making her explain what she didn't understand herself. "I wanted you, and you know it," she whispered, pride bringing a flush to her cheeks.

"On your terms."

"Why not? I don't let just any man into my life."

"Or your bed?"

Jennie remembered he could be as direct as she. "That too."

"Then why me? Why now? Maybe you've forgotten kicking me off the veranda. I said I needed you. I still do. I'm not going to lie for it, Jennie."

She sat back. If he wanted honesty, she'd give it to him. "I wanted you last night because I knew you'd be gone soon." She said it quickly, her dark eyes defiant.

"You can make love and let go that easily?"

"Who said anything about love?" For once her voice failed her and a flicker of doubt came through.

He pounced on it. "You can't, can you? If we made love it would mean as much to you as it would to me."

"Don't read anything into this, Jake."

Her request stopped him. He wanted her to want him. He'd had his fill of meaningless encounters since his divorce. Yet something told him her feelings weren't as inconsequential as she pretended. A voice inside him said, To hell with caution. For Jennie he'd risk it. He'd cross the line, commitment or no. And if, in the end, she decided against him, he'd accept the pain and go.

But first he'd make damn sure he had memories to take with him.

Six

"Let me show you what it means."

His kiss forced her head back. Their tongues dueled: his plunged, blatantly, suggestively; hers teased enticingly. They were standing now, and he was pulling her to his body so she could feel everything she'd done to him. Soon kissing wasn't enough. He was nibbling, biting, scraping his teeth down her neck, making her quiver in his arms.

Jennie knew it wasn't gratitude she felt, but it was more than physical need. She was letting him inside, when she'd let no one near her in the last two years. She couldn't hide from her emotions anymore. She wanted him in her life no matter how long he stayed. Sometimes loneliness demanded a high price. Like a parched tree in a drought, she would take his rain and make it last.

She wasn't wearing a bra. As he touched her something told him she never did. He'd seen her breasts before, rosy and recumbent in sleep. Now her nipples were like dark olives on her tanned skin, which was a deep-golden tone that went with her black hair and dark eyes. He pushed her shirt off her shoulders and just held it there. He watched the perspiration glimmer between her breasts, then he licked it away, transferring the salty moisture to the tip of one breast. It tightened and peaked as he held it between pursed lips. When he sucked, her hands coiled in his hair, and she moaned his name.

That was one, he thought. A memory he'd carry inside him as long as he lived, reverberating like a heartbeat. He taunted the other breast until she said his name again.

Shirts open, they pressed skin to skin. Jennie felt the heat, the dampness where they touched, the coolness of a belt buckle she had to undo. Jake stopped her hands, and their gazes locked for a long moment.

His calloused fingers traced the metal of her zipper, following the seam gently downward, rubbing softly at the apex of her thighs as she arched in response. He had to fight the urge to go fast, to bury himself inside her.

But first he had to endure her hand skimming his jeans, discovering his unmistakable hardness. He held himself taut, impatient, but his indrawn breath created a space for her hand to dip inside. When she touched him, he almost exploded. He'd been unaware of how exciting watching her had been for him. In another minute he'd be past stopping.

"Wait," he said suddenly, hoarsely. He circled her wrists with his large hands as the sound of an approaching truck reached them. "The men are back." His eyes were dark, his mouth grim.

They listened, staring into each other's eyes. It was no mistake. He cursed angrily and turned his back to button his shirt and tuck it in.

Jennie did the same, trying to hide her embarrassment with motion. She'd done it again. She'd flung herself at him for all the wrong reasons. Desperation. Greed. She'd been greedy to feel his touch, to be needed again.

When he stooped to pick up his discarded cowboy hat in the corner, she bolted. She had her pride, after all. It seemed that was all she had left.

With one quick stride he blocked the door. He didn't know how, but he'd half expected her to run. Maybe it was a good sign. Maybe it meant in a million years he'd understand her. "Wait."

The truck brakes whined to a halt, and men's voices could be heard clearly. For a minute Jake said nothing. Leaning against the door, his gaze locked with hers, he was breathing heavily, like a stallion at the end of a run. "Let me catch my breath before we go out there."

Her gaze broke from his, unconsciously sweeping his body. It was obvious why he wanted to wait. She lifted her chin and with immense effort tried to achieve some distance, some dignity. "I can make my own way to the house."

He let her step through the door, but his hand caught her arm before she got any farther. "It was a bad time, Jennie."

"Is there such a thing as a good time for us? Maybe we're going about this all wrong, Jake. You need me, and I can't give you anything in return. All I can do is use you."

"Let me be the judge of that." He loosened his grip, and she started walking. "Tonight, Jennie."

He said it so softly, she stopped three steps away, afraid to turn, afraid to go on. Afraid of the torture of an evening of not knowing whether he meant what he'd said or not. Was she only hearing what she wanted to hear? She knew she wouldn't deny him if he came to her. They were too combustible together. But she couldn't ask him to repeat what he'd said, and she didn't think she could bear an evening of waiting to find out.

What would either of them gain from a casual encounter? She had to put distance between them, find some control over her dizzying emotions.

The men came in, their boots sounding hard on the creaking wooden floor. They stopped in surprise, their gazes darting from Jennie to Jake, standing in the doorway of his room.

She swallowed hard and drew enough breath to project her voice. "I wanted to thank you all for today." She willed herself to step forward and put out her hand. "You're Burt, aren't you?"

"Yes, ma'am."

She shook his hand. "Thank you, Burt. Your sharp hearing saved my life." She saw her truck parked in the drive beside the yellow one the men used, and seized the excuse to step outside. "Could any of you tell me if the groceries were saved too?" She forced a smile.

A man jumped on the running board and rifled through the sacks. "Most of it looks good. Real good." He whistled as he saw the steaks.

Jennie laughed, genuinely relieved, and turned to address the men. The sight of Jake in the doorway of the bunkhouse was a distraction she couldn't allow to affect her. "Considering how hot it was in that truck, I think those steaks had better be cooked immediately. So, I'd like to invite all of you to a barbecue behind the house tonight at seven. It's the least I can do. Your being here really has been a godsend, and I appreciate what you're doing."

"The men have a date with a fire," Jake said, his voice gruff. "Dawn tomorrow morning."

Several of the men groaned, but Jennie sensed this was routine. "Then I promise not to keep them up too late." She was on center stage now, a part she knew how to play well. She addressed the group gathered around her. "We'll have a cookout: steak, salads, wine, and beer. If that's okay with your boss." She tilted her head in Jake's direction.

The men smiled and waited. They knew he wouldn't refuse her offer. "Beer's okay," he said by way of permission. The men cheered.

Jennie felt hot and flushed all over, her body tingling inside her clothes. She was wired with energy, and it took every ounce of it she possessed to ignore the way Jake was watching her. He stared as if he could see right through her blouse to the flesh he'd sucked moments before. If he only knew how her breasts still felt the imprint of his lips. "Oh, and music," Jennie said, thinking on her feet, distracting herself as much as she could. "We can't have a party without music. Bring along some of your tapes."

"The Jennie Cisco tape?" one of them suggested.

"No, the John Denver!" she shot back. Everyone laughed. By then she'd reached the front steps of the house, her knees weak. She opened the door for the men carrying the groceries. "Thanks, guys. Tonight."

Tonight. Jake had said the word. She hadn't imagined it. In fact, she'd stood there and quoted it to his men. The furious look on his face as she closed the screen door was all the confirmation she'd needed. He'd think she was doing nothing but putting people between them. Maybe she was. Maybe distance was exactly what they needed in order to cool down.

But if he did mean to come to her that night, what better way to make the hours go faster? she thought.

She fussed in the kitchen, preparing everything that could be fixed beforehand, then took a long bath, vigorously rinsing her hair. At first she thought the smokiness would never wash away. Now hanging free and wild, her hair smelled clean, and she had no desire to braid it again. She'd let it dry in the wind in what little breeze there was. If the evening was as muggy as the afternoon, the lingering dampness might last for hours. Maybe it would keep her cool, calm down the heat-induced case of nerves she was experiencing.

The men were getting ready too. One by one they showered the smoke and sweat away under the trough hose. As they drifted over to the barbecue, Jennie noticed each was freshly scrubbed and shaved. She got the feeling they'd enjoyed getting rid of the pine-tar smell as much as she had.

Coming around the shady side of the house, each man tipped his cowboy hat shyly as he appeared. A low whistle from one of them earned a warning look from Chick as Jennie set the salad fixings on the picnic table. The older man seemed to have appointed himself charcoal starter and unofficial spokesman for the group. "Thanks for the invite, ma'am."

"Make yourselves at home," she said brightly. Offering to fetch drinks, she settled in as hostess. Jake had yet to appear. It gave her a few minutes to catch her breath.

"I had second thoughts about grilling," she said, laughing with appealing self-consciousness. "After today I wasn't sure I ever wanted to smell smoke again. But mesquite is a little different."

"Smells mighty fine to me," one man piped up. The others agreed.

"As long as we don't start any fires with it," another added.

"Hey, Chick, think you can get those coals started all by yourself?"

"Maybe we should dig a line around it." Everyone laughed.

It was a small group, but a jovial one. Soon Jennie knew all the men's names, their hometowns, and the appeal fire fighting held for each of them. Comfortable with each other from long experience and shared dangers, they were easy to like, and Jennie wondered more than once why she'd been denying herself company for so long.

Yet in spite of the relaxed atmosphere, she was keenly aware that Jake hadn't arrived.

Chick called out to a man going in the back door, "Grab me another beer while you're in there, Greg, and don't track dirt in the lady's house. When Jake gets here he'll chew you out but good."

Greg grumbled while the others laughed. Jennie caught Chick's eye, aware that his comment about Jake's imminent arrival was for her benefit. A knot of tension between her shoulder blades softened, while the tension of anticipation began.

Someone slipped another tape in the machine, and a collection of soothing love songs filtered through the evening air. Chick declared himself chief steak flipper. The men helped set up the various dishes and took their places in line as Jennie served.

"Serve yourself first, Miss Cisco. These guys can help themselves," Chick said.

"I don't mind."

"See? She doesn't mind."

"Yeah, Chick. We've had you dishin' out our food for a month—let a pretty lady do it, for a change."

Then he was there. Jennie was spooning out cole slaw. She didn't look up—something told her not to—but she knew. Her heart beat faster, an erratic percussion that had become normal around Jake. She swung the ladle wide, and a clump of slaw ended up on the picnic table instead of a plate.

"I'm sorry," she said, and laughed uncomfortably, glancing at the man in front of her, taking the chance to watch Jake lean against the corner of the house, his arms crossed on his chest. Her smile faded. It was an effort to tear her gaze away from his brooding blue eyes.

Why? Why did he even want her? She'd been as prickly as a cactus since they'd first met. Why was she apprehensive when he was gone, all nerves the minute he arrived?

"Come over here and get a plate, Jake," Chick called. "You're gonna miss out on all these fixin's."

Jake pushed himself away from the house and sauntered over with a laid-back stride, too self-contained to be a swagger, too blatantly masculine to be ignored. Jennie could feel his gaze boring into her. Concentrating on the food, she refused to look up. They moved down the table together. At the end of the line she set a muffin on his plate. "Is that enough?"

"You know it isn't." With the terse reply, he walked away.

She filled her own plate defiantly high and took a seat at the table. It wasn't long before the men asked about her career. Although she tensed for a moment, she soon found it wasn't too difficult to talk about that period in her life so far in the past. The anecdotes flowed, of hotel horrors, of doing ten shows in ten days in ten states, of famous acquaintances, and of how she wrote the songs.

"What about groupies?"

Jennie's smile was replaced with a chilly look. On the bench by the house, Jake sat up a little straighter. "I don't call them groupies," she said sharply.

The men traded glances, the conversation slowed.

"They're just kids, most of them. Girls who don't receive the love or the discipline they need at home. They're looking for status, self-esteem, something to convince them they're somebody. They think getting on the bus means getting in the business. They hope some of the stardust will rub off, and they'll be special too." She shook her head sadly. "Most of all they want attention. They need love, like everybody else."

The men considered what she'd said, while Jennie wondered if she ought to apologize for lecturing. So many people didn't know what went on in the music business. Either they were caught up in the glamour and meticulously planned image-mongering, or they believed every grimy drug and sex rumor they heard.

Jennie rubbed her forehead. Now she was lecturing herself.

The party picked up as the sun sank behind the mountain peaks. The batteries on the tape player grew weak, and Jennie invited the men inside, ignoring the dark looks Jake aimed her way.

He ambled in last. He'd seen the house, the kitchen, the cavernous living room with the massive stone fireplace. The house always had seemed dark when he'd entered after being in the harsh sunlight outside, but lit up at night, it was something else. Lights shone on the polished wood floor, bringing out the colors in the hanging Indian rugs and woven pillows on the couch. It was obvious Jennie liked color—rich, earthy, and bold. Like the woman he knew she was. Obviously she'd made enough money in her career never to have to worry about bills, or car repairs, or child-support payments.

Jake had become financially comfortable only over the last couple of years, since he'd added computer work to his fire-fighting skills and become something of a specialist. Jennie Cisco probably had had more money than she could spend for quite some time. He wondered if she remembered what it was like on the other side of the fence. The thought served to widen the gulf between them.

He took a swig of beer and watched her move around the room, smiling and laughing. The hair falling around her shoulders made her look like a Madonna. If he'd been staring at her when he first came around the house, it was because he'd never seen her hair free. It was kinked from constant braiding, thick and wild, covering her shoulders like a midnight cape. It suited the passionate side of her, the sensual woman, full and ripe and ready for a man.

With olive skin, dark eyes, and a wide mouth set at a stubborn angle in a face that was otherwise delicate, Jennie could have been Indian—maybe Mexican. Was Cisco her real name or a stage name? he wondered. He'd never thought to ask her. What else didn't he know?

Yet there he sat, his gut twisting while she looked at everyone but him, waiting for a chance to take her to bed. Was he a fool? For a woman who was ready—damn eager, at times—she certainly wasn't making it easy for him. She'd started by shutting him out of her life, trying to run him off her land. Suddenly she'd discovered she could keep him at bay by surrounding herself with people. So be it. He could wait. But he didn't have to enjoy it.

Joe ran a hand over the deep polish on the baby grand piano, listening to the squeak of his hand on the mahogany. "Bet that cost a pretty penny."

"Behave yourself," Jake said. He looked directly at Jennie. It was the first time she'd let him catch her eye all evening. "If you guys can't be polite, I'll order you all to bed," he said in a low voice, with a twist of a smile.

The men took his comment good-naturedly. She didn't. With a lurch in her stomach, she realized she wasn't putting anything off. If he wanted to, Jake could ensure they'd be alone. He only had to say the word.

He smiled thinly and sipped his beer.

One of the men tinkled the piano keys, humming as he poked out a melody. His attempt was met by groans, and he was soon shouted down.

"Play something else."

"Play a real song."

"Learn to play!"

Jennie joined in the laughter. Whether she was avoiding Jake or not, she was enjoying herself. She had a few fans in the group. She'd been cornered in the kitchen and asked to autograph the tape of her greatest hits, but no one was grasping, or hounding her. Instead she felt surrounded by friends, relaxation mixed with a twinge of regret. For the sake of protecting her precious privacy, she'd been missing out on this kind of camaraderie.

And a chance with a man like Jake was something she'd been missing all her life. What if he'd taken her up on her first reaction to him and never come back to the ranch? He hadn't. Now the question was, what if he stayed the night? How quickly fate turned the tables! she thought.

Making love with Jake would mean everything to her. It would turn her solitary world upside down, shatter every wall she'd built. It would also mean love, she thought, glancing at her reflection in the dark window. Life could begin again.

Suddenly, her name broke through the haze. "Jennie, you play."

She and Jake looked up from different sides of the room.

"I mean, Miss Cisco, if you wouldn't mind, that is."

Jennie braced herself. The panic and discomfort she'd felt in the grocery store didn't return. She smiled instead. "I haven't played in public for ages, guys."

"We're not public."

"Naw."

"Go ahead. Or if you don't want to sing, you play 'Montana' and we'll sing."

"I heard you singing it last night." She laughed, making a face.

Jake had never seen her so relaxed. For a long second he resented the smiles she gave so easily to everyone but him.

She stepped toward the piano, urged forward, nearer to where Jake was leaning against the back of the sofa, his long legs straight in front of him, crossed at the ankles.

"Please?"

"Just one song."

She shook her head emphatically, her loose hair

casting cool blue highlights as it whispered over her shoulders. Jake caught the whiff of apricot shampoo and lingering dampness. He wanted to take handfuls of her hair and press them to his face. He held the beer can so tightly, he dented it.

Jennie was losing the argument, but her rejoinders were growing less genuine. "I don't know if I can sing more than one. I haven't kept my voice in shape. I just write, nowadays."

"You must sing them when you write them."

"I just hum the words." She demonstrated, hunched comically over the keys, plucking out notes and murmuring words and melody so low, every man in the room leaned forward, laughing.

"Come on."

"Sing something."

Jake's voice was husky and quiet, but it cut through the gaggle of voices with soft, undeniable command. "Do it for real, Jennie."

Their gazes locked. How long it lasted, she couldn't say. She couldn't say anything for a minute. Her throat was dry, her lips in a tight line. He was challenging her in front of everyone, propositioning her for everyone to hear. How could they not know? It was as obvious as the flush on her cheeks and the trembling of her hands.

She had to play now, if only to keep her fingers busy. "Tell you what," she said brightly, "one of you had a good idea. I'll play, *you* sing." Before they could protest, she started the familiar opening bars of "Montana."

The men joined in eagerly, pausing as one at the bridge, although they wouldn't have known what to call it. The bridge was the high, soaring part in the middle, the part her voice carried and floated over, her tremulous contralto catching each man's heart in a longing for home: "A home we'll share, only home when you're here . . ."

The room got quiet. Jennie finished out the song by herself, each man lost in his own thoughts, Chick nodding to himself, Joe sipping his beer, Burt stroking the end of his mustache. When the last notes died out, they remembered to applaud.

"Bravo."

"Another."

"No, thanks. The songs I write now you wouldn't know. The old songs I haven't played in years."

"I'll put on your greatest hits, then you'll remember."

"No, no, don't do that. It makes me nervous to hear myself sing." But not half as nervous as she expected, she realized. She cleared her throat and took a sip of ice water. A small audience was still an audience. She was treading on slippery ground, but her voice felt good, the butterflies manageable. Her hands still shook, but they hit the right keys. "I'll take a stab at one more."

She sang another. Then another. She told herself she was taking no big risk. The familiarity of the group was her safety net, but it was farther out of her self-imposed exile than she'd gone in two years. If this was the edge, she'd see how far she could walk.

A sampling of her greatest hits followed, songs that were theirs more than hers. Then she sang "When You Were There." It was a love song. The recording was composed of her voice and the stark, sultry pleading of a piano. To some of the men it was as if a record had come to life—to Jake it was a window.

She was singing to him, as corny as he knew that might sound. He wouldn't have admitted it to anyone in a million years, but he believed it as firmly as he believed they were in the same room. She was laying it out before him; the vulnerability beneath the prickly facade, strong on the outside because the inside was so fragile; living in the past and knowing it would never be enough; the wasted years; the honesty to face it all; the willingness to try again.

Jennie heard it too; it was impossible to sing without conveying everything she felt. Too much was coming through in her voice, but she couldn't stop. It was the song, she told herself, it was a good one. It could hold the emotion she gave it, shape her words, express and amplify every feeling. This wasn't a song she'd written for someone else, not like those she'd sent out lately, imagining what good, poor, or mediocre performers would make of them. This was her song, and she could fill it with the passion over something lost, never to be regained. It would take and accept and communicate. And she wanted so badly to communicate.

The song ended. She played out the last bars, watching her hands moving over the keys. The applause was scattered around the room, with murmurings of approval. She was afraid to look up, to see what emotion waited in Jake's eyes. Recognition? Triumph?

Suddenly she heard his low voice. "Time to hit the road, guys."

Her gaze flew to him, so arrogant was his response. This wasn't his party to break up.

But the men were leaving dutifully. Jennie stood stiffly at the door, trying her damnedest to play hostess, when all she wanted to do was to throw something at Jake's head. How dare he break up her party! The sheer audacity of the man!

One by one the men shook her hand and thanked her for the evening. She'd made eleven new friends, but not one of them could help her out of the dilemma she'd gotten herself into. In a moment she'd be alone with Jake, and she was totally unsure of how to handle the situation.

Chick paused on the steps. "Coming, Jake?"

"I'll be along in a minute."

"I have cleaning up to do," Jennie said sharply, making it clear his staying or going mattered not at all to her. She retreated hastily to the kitchen.

Beer cans stood on the counter. Mixing bowls and cutlery filled the sink. She had to get to work on it. Can't let this stuff sit out all night, she told herself.

"You hiding in here?"

"I am not." The denial was automatic, her voice firm, but he couldn't hear what her body was saying. She slammed a pan on the counter. She was flustered and angry, and she didn't know why.

"You're angry."

"Are you really going to be so blatant about staying?"

"You're worried about what my men will think?"

She turned both faucets on full blast. "Obviously you don't know what it's like having your name splashed all over the tabloids. Not that anyone cares anymore. But living on the edge of a small town doesn't help. I'm sensitive to how things look." She squirted a mound of detergent into the rising water.

"It looks like what it is. I planned on staying." Jake came up behind her and touched her. She jumped as if branded. "That's not what you're angry about. You're scared."

"I've got dishes to do." Her lines were going from abysmal to worse. How flustered could she get? Even with her back to him, she was aware of how he was standing with one knee bent, how strong and taut and sturdy his legs were. She caught the faint masculine smell of him, of soap and some kind of woodsy after-shave.

"Come on, Jennie," he said in an insinuating voice that would have done the devil proud, "it isn't like you to hide."

She grimaced. No it wasn't, but she'd been doing a lot of it lately. Out of the corner of her eye she saw his chest expand as he breathed, and she felt hers contract. When she caught sight of his large hands turning a plate over, rubbing it with the dishcloth, her heart pounded.

"Well?" he asked. "I'd rather have you hissing at me; at least I'd know where I stand. You were singing to me tonight. No one's ever done that." He touched her hair, filled his hand with it. He'd wanted to do it all night. There were a lot of things he'd wanted for a long time. The knot in his stomach told him he was on the edge of doing them or losing them forever. "Why are you afraid? Is it because I said I need you? That's been a burr under your saddle all along."

"Don't," she said in a strangled voice.

He ran his fingers over her scalp, pulling her hair back, skimming the ridges of her ears. "Don't you need, too, Jennie?"

Her hands were shaking so hard, the silverware clattered into the sudsy water. She gripped the edge of the sink. It was porcelain, cool to the touch, but her hands were sudsy and wet, and she could feel her grip slipping.

Don't you need, too? Her honest reply? Yes, yes, yes. Her life was empty. Surrounding herself with people was nice, refreshing, but letting him in—that was too naked a need. "I'd let you down."

"Why?"

"If you needed me, I might not be there for you."

"I'm a big boy. I can take care of myself."

"You don't understand. I might be so wrapped up in being the great helper that I wouldn't listen. I've got an ego, Jake."

"Don't we all?"

"Mine's been stroked more than most."

"Like this?" he asked as he caressed her breasts.

She shuddered and moaned. "You don't play fair."

"I'm not playing." He lifted her magnificent hair out of the way and kissed the back of her neck. "I'd call this serious business, this love stuff."

Seven

She stiffened and tried to turn, shaking her head. No, oh, no, she thought. The last thing she wanted was to hurt him. He was getting in too deep, and she couldn't promise him anything. "Jake, please."

"Let me love you, that's all I ask. When I said *need* I didn't mean I would be dependent on you. What I really need, Jennie, is for you to let me in." He kissed the back of her neck again, softly sealing his words. "I think that's what we both need."

She leaned against his shoulder, feeling his eager touch everywhere. He made her quiver and grow weak. She was desperately trying to think, and he kept distracting her. A dozen questions tumbled through her mind, all of which her body would have answered with yes, yes. Whatever cautions her brain supplied were quickly forgotten. Like stones in a pond, her doubts sank quickly, leaving nothing but ripples and warnings behind, fading, fading and sinking. There were her needs to consider—yes, she needed too.

She touched him then, her fingers alert to the

warmth and stubble of his cheek, her gaze to the dark hunger of his. The sudsy water made her fingers slick as she compared the smoothness of ivory piano keys to the texture of a man's skin. A cluster of bubbles clung to her wrist. He blew on them softly, and they tingled as they burst and dissolved.

His hands were rough on the curve of her back. Her skin had never felt so silky to her until calluses like his touched it. She wanted to compare her cheek to the swirling hair on his chest, her lips to the pounding vein on his neck, her still-slick fingers to the satiny hot skin she'd found below his belt that afternoon, the touch that had made him rigid. Slowly she unfastened the next two buttons of his shirt.

"Jake?"

The man's voice startled them both. Jennie jumped, but Jake's hold was like iron. He turned his head, his voice gruff. "Yeah, Greg, what do you want?"

"Got a call on the field radio. The sheriff has some rangers coming in for a meeting. He wants you there. Tonight."

"May I use your phone?"

"By the sofa," she said, wiping clinging tendrils of hair off her neck. She glared at both men's backs, while Greg chose to stare at a Navajo rug and Jake dialed the sheriff's number. Anxious and restless, Jennie absently braided her hair.

Jake mumbled into the phone. His words to Greg as he hung up were clearer. "Get my Jeep."

"It's right outside." The young man held the door open.

For a moment Jake wanted to damn efficiency in all its forms. "Then give us a minute, will you?"

"Sure." The screen door slammed as Greg got out fast. "Sorry," he called from the drive.

Jake stood in the kitchen doorway, stuck his hands in his back pockets, and foundered for a few seconds. Jennie stood still, thinking how much she hated waiting.

"I'll be in town a few hours."

"Go ahead, go."

He wanted so badly to touch her again. Inwardly he cursed everything that got in the way with her. "Maybe I'll pick up a little something in town," he said.

She finished her braid and flung it over her shoulder. Whether she meant to or not, she could shut him out so easily. He wondered if she knew that.

"Do they have an all-night drugstore in Lone Pine?"

"For what?"

"For me to get something to protect you."

A look of surprise registered on her face. Jennie glanced at the screen door and the man silhouetted in the driveway. "Don't you think it would be obvious to your driver?"

"I'll say I've got a headache."

She tried to salvage some humor from the situation. "That should be my line."

"It won't be."

No, it wouldn't be, she thought.

"The men will know eventually, especially when I start spending all my spare time with you."

Jennie tried to ignore the flash of pleasure she felt. After all, he wasn't proposing anything permanent, just killing time. "Didn't know you had any to spare."

"Mostly my nights."

The Jeep started with a roar.

"Go to your meeting," she said quietly, returning to her dishes. It wasn't polite, and it probably was a bad sign, but she didn't want to stand there and watch him leave.

She scrubbed forks with a vengeance. Not wanting her privacy invaded in any way, here she was about to have her love life revealed to a dozen men. She dropped a plate and jumped at the crash. Whisk broom in hand, she cursed the plate, the kitchen floor, the heat, and anything else that came to mind short of Jake Kramer. She didn't need this kind of aggravation.

Why had he ever come along? And why did her heart insist on feeling so empty when he was gone? A loneliness she thought she'd conquered long ago had returned in the last few days. "Let me in, Jennie," he'd said. He already was in.

Dishes put away, the house dark, she walked out onto the veranda. The moon had gone down, and she looked at the deep black night dotted by a thousand piercing stars. A miniature light show, she thought, lighted matches from a crowd of thousands screaming for an encore. Did he have any conception of her world? Did she of his? Did any of it matter, when she wanted him so badly?

She remembered the fear she'd felt earlier that afternoon. She could still see a truck's dashboard, dust in the crevices of its cracked vinyl, a peeling state park sticker on the window. And she quickly thought of two years of a life put on hold. She wanted to live again. But that involved Jake, and he wasn't there.

Later, sitting on the sofa, gazing through the screen, she watched lights flicker out in the bunk-house. She rearranged some pillows, set her chin on her crossed arms, and waited. Lord, how she hated waiting.

It was dawn. She'd been dreaming about a tall blond man standing outside her screen door, about hot things, pictures and sensations that made her twist in her sleep. The sound of his shout woke her like a siren.

He was standing in the drive, directing traffic, getting the men off for the morning. There were more people now, half a dozen new men in ranger uniforms, she realized.

But none of that mattered. Jake had come back during the night and he hadn't come to her. It was astonishing how much she hurt. But she'd be damned if she'd continue to lie on the couch as if she'd been waiting for him. She coughed up an acrid taste from the day before and went upstairs to brush her teeth. Then she stalked into the kitchen, incensed with herself for having all the dishes done and nothing to busy herself with. She wished Glaze were there to groom or feed. She'd make breakfast, she decided. A small thing like her total lack of appetite wasn't going to stop her.

She flung the refrigerator door open and tossed a handful of blindly chosen ingredients onto the counter. A minute later he was standing in the doorway, watching her break eggs. "Didn't you go to bed last night?"

She was disheveled and exhausted, and she needed a cup of strong coffee. She didn't want a confrontation; she wanted to be left alone. A tiny voice inside her said, *It would have happened anyway. He'd leave and you'd be alone. Better to face it now.*

"I went to sleep." She shrugged, avoiding the cool stare he aimed her way.

"Move over. I'll make the coffee." He practically elbowed her out of the way, heedless of her fiery look. "Hope you don't mind my helping myself to your kitchen." He knew she'd mind plenty. Invasion of her privacy was sure to get her riled up. He even grinned. No way was she shutting him out again, he vowed to himself.

Jennie caught on quickly. If he thought she'd give him the satisfaction of an argument . . . "Make yourself right at home." She gestured grandly, muttering into her empty cup, "You already have." She marched into the living room and plopped herself down on the couch.

A few minutes later Jake nudged her feet aside to sit down. He concentrated on the strong coffee, and not on the way she curled her legs under her as far as they would go. "Didn't know if you'd want eggs too."

She realized she'd left three broken ones sitting in a bowl. She'd been caught running again. "If you're hungry, fix it yourself."

Obviously he was more tired than hungry; the few glances she spared him told her as much. His shirt was stiff with dried sweat and reeked of smoke, his hands were half black around his coffee mug, and his face was smudged. The deep crinkles around his eyes looked carved. Suddenly she felt guilty. He'd been fighting the fire all night, and she'd jumped all over him before he could explain.

"If you'd like to take a shower . . ." Her offer died in her throat. She took another drink, marveled at how strong he'd made it, and tried again. "Think you can find the shower?"

Jake didn't answer. It wasn't much of an offer, and she didn't make it sound very friendly. "I know where the horse trough is."

A look he'd be flattered to call hurt flitted through her eyes as she stared into the impenetrable coffee. "I meant mine. Off the loft, up there."

She should have known he'd make things difficult. After the cold shoulder she'd given him when he came in, she didn't really blame him.

Stretching an arm along the back of the couch, he toyed with her braid. "Join me?" He could tell by the tension in her neck as his hand closed on it, rubbing softly, that his offer surprised her. "Aw, hell, Jennie." He set down his cup, then hers, producing a splash of brown on the white marble end table.

Their mouths tasted like hot coffee, but the flavor dissolved quickly, and she was aware of the dark masculine pungency of him. Slowly, gradually, he was leaning back. Her hair was half braided, half loose, long tendrils skimming her cheeks and his as he pulled her down. As in her dream, she was falling. No matter how she ordered her eyes to open, they wouldn't. Her body was too intent on sensations, the tug of his mouth, the exploring thrust of his tongue, the feel of his cheek scraping hers when he sought the skin of her neck and kissed a trail from her ear to her sensitive collarbone. His hands were toughened by work. The scratchy, hard feel of him made her feel softer, more feminine . . .

"You're so soft," he said, cupping her chin in his hand.

. . . and the way he picked up on feelings she thought were hidden, made her feel frighteningly vulnerable.

He rubbed a smudge off her chin. "I shouldn't be

touching you like this. Now you really will have to join me in the shower." He traced her cheekbone.

She shivered. Something about the touch of his dirty hand against her cheek caused a faint flush beneath her smudged skin.

"I'm sorry my hands are dirty. I should have brought you better."

He stared into her eyes, and she saw the look she feared. The look in his eyes was more than fire, more than lust. It was apology, need, a rough vulnerability all his own. "You don't owe me anything, Jake."

"You should have the best money can buy."

"Then I'll buy it myself." She tried to lift herself off him, aware of exactly how far she'd fallen. Want, need, love—how could she know which was which when he touched her?

"You can't buy what I can give you," he said. Suddenly he took her mouth in a searing kiss. Then he found her ear, his tongue making her gasp and arch against him.

"Don't."

He laughed out loud, his body shaking underneath her, making her feel things she didn't want to feel. "We already are, darlin'."

She pushed against him, but the fury deserted her as soon as her hand touched his rock-hard chest. It was a mistake, lingering over the feel of him while trying to get away. He was hard all over, and her squirming was a futile deterrent. His arms circled her waist in a barely disguised vise.

"Let me go, Jake." Her voice was flat now, her brown eyes cold. Her hands were fists on his chest.

"So you're making all the decisions for us."

"There is no us." Jennie's gaze remained on the coffee mug she needed both hands to hold.

He continued as if he hadn't heard her, glad her face couldn't be hidden from him by her flowing hair. "You decided I could want but not need. You named the terms."

"I think that's my prerogative."

"I have a say in our relationship too, Jennie."

"Well, I have something to say, Jake Kramer." She gulped and looked him straight in the eye. "You make the lousiest coffee I have ever tasted."

He wasn't going to be sidetracked by wisecracks. "Is that all?" His steady look cut through her, and he watched her resolve crumble just a little.

"Why didn't you come home last night?"

Home. Part of him jumped at the word, part heard the hurt in her voice she tried so hard to play down, part of him finally understood. "I thought it was obvious." He spread his smoke-stained hands.

She took a deep breath, scrunched her shoulders up toward her ears, and exhaled with a rush. Then she smiled at him, a smile Jake had never seen before, a warm, happy, everything's-fine smile. Somehow it went with the word *home.* He was home, and she could relax.

She patted him on the knee and headed off toward the kitchen feeling one hundred percent better. "Take your shower, cowboy. You smell like the fireplace."

Jake wrapped a towel around himself and wadded his clothes into the washing machine in the alcove off the bathroom.

Running water in the kitchen, Jennie heard the cycle start and shook her head. He certainly did know how to make himself at home, she thought. She wasn't prepared, however, when he walked into the kitchen wearing nothing but a light blue towel, one that matched his eyes, she noted.

She wasn't a schoolgirl—she was a grown woman. She knew what was under the towel. The fact that it was making her quiver like a teenager was the galling part.

Jake waited. Under the cold, hard spray of the shower some things had become clear to him. He'd thought about her while at the fire—the passion hidden in shooting flames, the mystery in plumes of smoke curling upward until they obliterated even the stars. He wanted to tell her she'd been on his mind. Then he thought of how all the plans a man made could go up in smoke, in the flash of lightning striking a tree somewhere on a mountaintop. And when Chick had spelled him, he'd drunk from his canteen and thought of one more thing: She'd be there when he got back. That had made all the difference. She was important to him. Everywhere he went she was inside him. He'd wait for her.

"Are you going to stand there in that towel?"

"My clothes are in the wash."

"So I noticed."

He grinned at her petulant tone. She couldn't be indifferent to him, he was sure. "I could come over and help dry." He started to unwrap the towel.

"Don't you dare."

He chuckled and came up beside her, kissing the back of her neck, sliding one arm around her waist, his thumb tracing the underside of her breast. Jennie froze. If he made her drop a plate she'd scream. She was a bundle of nerves as it was. It was barely seven A.M., and the day was already hot.

He could feel her tension. "I want to touch you, Jennie. Don't say no."

She could have argued with a demand, rebuffed a seductive line. But she couldn't fight his quiet request. He bent his head to kiss her. Rising on her toes, she met him halfway, and what started gently became an overture to lovemaking, his tongue thrusting into her sweetness, her mouth opening and closing around him until their bodies were inflamed and frustrated by their mocking imitation of the real thing. She smelled the soap on him, the dampness. His skin was flecked with moisture, droplets clinging to the hairs on his chest, and her hands practically squeaked against the skin on his back. He bent her backward until her body curved to every contour of his. Still it wasn't enough.

She'd never felt this way with any other man, she realized. He was fire and she was tinder. He made her hiss and burn and burst into flame. He'd never made her feel cool, indifferent. The inevitability of it all made her wonder briefly what twist of fate had brought him to her ranch—and when fate would take him away.

But fate could be stalled.

"I want you," she whispered, looking up into his blue eyes.

He nodded. "Upstairs."

He'd seen the loft when he went up to shower. A Japanese screen blocked the bedroom from the downstairs. There was a large bed framed in driftwood, with a homemade quilt. He'd noted the soft colors, the white turned-down sheets she hadn't slept on the previous night. Stripping before stepping into the cool spray, feeling half dead from the tough night, his first thought had been how good it would feel to sleep in a real bed. The mental picture had come to him swiftly of Jennie on those sheets, and the tiredness had left him. The ache hadn't.

He stepped back and took her hands in his, leading her up the stairs. It was like a furnace, hot and dry. They could feel the temperature rise with every step. At the foot of the bed he let the towel drop to the floor, and they stood looking at each other.

With one fluid move, she ran her hands down him, then up, murmuring how beautiful he was, and, in case he misunderstood, how strong. She lifted her blouse over her head and let it fall at his feet.

It was his turn to speak—soft, disjointed words of wonder. She felt his rough hands in the waistband of her peasant skirt. He left the silk bikini panties on her, relishing the feel of his hand on her waist, then silk, her thigh, then silk again. The backs of his fingers stroked her abdomen and the fullness of her breasts.

His voice was low. "I've seen you naked before. Why is it different every time?" She started to speak. He stopped her with a kiss. Holding her face in his hands, he peered into her eyes, which were deep as wells, the kind where wishes are made. "Never mind. I get the feeling I'll never understand what happens between us. If we could explain it, maybe it'd be easier—maybe it wouldn't be as good. I don't think you'll ever be easy, Jennie, but you will be mine."

Their mouths joined, his hands riffling through her hair as his fingers unwound it. Only for him would she be this pliant, letting him touch, taste, and take from her. Only for him would her hair spread on the pillow like a black mane as he coaxed her back on the bed.

The sheets were cool but the room was hot. Everywhere their bodies touched they were wet. He held himself over her on straightened arms. She smiled in an unabashedly seductive way, pursed her lips around one of his nipples, and bit it softly. His moan met a reply deep in her throat. The sound was something between a growl and a purr. With her fingertips she strummed the muscles of his rib cage, her fingernails tracing individual hairs, following the path downward into the soft, damp curls that surrounded his manhood. She touched him there, and his arms quaked with effort.

"Jennie," he ground out between clenched teeth.

He was so beautiful, she wanted to throw back her head and laugh with joy. With the perspiration glistening on his body, the veins on his muscled arms pulsing, the reined-in force she so fearlessly called forth, he was beautiful. His gaze locked with hers, and she stroked him deep down where she couldn't see him, wantonly drawing one foot up the back of his leg, her hand encircling him with rhythmic caresses.

With a groan he sank to his elbows. "Do you need these?" he asked, one hand gripping the edge of her panties. She ignored him at her peril, and the panties snapped, a tiny mound of champagne-colored silk cast among the sheets. The woman was a temptress, a goddess of fire who had him burning. If she only knew how she controlled him now. . . .

His hand sought to even the ante, and her smile vanished. No longer did she taunt him with her power. Hot and wet, her hidden places opened to him. In dazzling seconds he taught her how little she knew about true wantonness. Everything he did drove her higher. As her neck arced in reckless desire, he seized her with his mouth, devouring her breasts as she pressed into his embrace.

Nothing happened slowly after that. Shining with

sweat, their bodies slid together with slick pressure and stunning friction, and he was filling her and she was whispering his name and licking a bead of sweat from his cheek. Her hips strained upward in a plea for him to move deeper and higher, and hotter and faster, and she shivered even though she felt as if she were on fire. Choking back sobs, she drifted alone on a plateau that quaked around her, until his plunging thrust, his hoarse shout of her name told her she wasn't alone. He was with her, so deep inside her he would always be there, always be there.

Eight

It was as if the world had stopped and they were in the center of it. They lay quietly. No air moved. Even with the windows open, it was stuffy in the loft. Vaguely Jennie wondered when she'd slept there last. For days she'd used the spare room off the veranda—the previous night, the sofa. After years of motels, hotels, and buses, she cherished her own bed. But it never would be hers alone again. Jake's memory would share it with her. With an aching heart, she wondered how many memories they'd make before he was gone.

What good was love if it had to end? But what was life without it? Jake had given her life new meaning, and she'd keep his love close and safe inside her—if she couldn't keep him.

He was too heavy. It was too hot. Jake lifted himself off her, surprised when she reached up to bring him back. "I'm not going," he said softly, stretching out beside her on one elbow. He watched a drop of water slide down one rosy breast. "Now you're the one who needs a shower."

"Join me?" A slow smile curled the corners of her mouth.

He lay back and stared at the beamed ceiling. Shouting for joy right now wouldn't be the smartest of moves. Instead he bit his tongue and squeezed her fingers between his. Kissing her hand, he couldn't subdue a grin.

"Men!" she said in a huffy tone.

He wasn't sure what her teasing summation meant, so he merely raised an eyebrow.

"I see that self-satisfied smirk, Mr. Kramer."

"Oooh." He winced. "We're on a last-name basis now, are we?" A laugh broke through. "So I'm happy. Shouldn't I be?" He kissed her hand again with a loud smack. "I think this is reason to celebrate."

"I think it's a typical male reaction to getting what you've been after." Her teasing tone might have acted as camouflage, but Jake understood the subtext.

Damn, damn, damn, he thought. She was pulling away again. He couldn't panic; he'd keep it light, follow her lead. "Aren't you being kind of cynical?"

"I'm trying to be a realist." He'd never know how hard she was trying.

"Typical cynic's response."

She frowned, at a loss for a comeback. If only she could let herself believe they had a chance. Was that why she was reducing their relationship to its lowest level? Because he hadn't expressed any intention of sticking around? She didn't think so. People moved on; she couldn't keep a man who didn't want to be kept. Enjoy the moments, tuck them away, and treasure them later, she told herself.

He kicked the sheet from where it clung to his ankles. When he spoke, the simple pleasure of lying together drained away. "Why can't you just be happy?"

She rolled over on her side, remembering all too

well the people who had loved her as an ideal, an image, for the qualities they'd imagined she possessed. She had to make him see who she really was, before he needed things she couldn't deliver, before he got hurt.

"Are you afraid this is all I wanted?" His voice was patient, understanding. He ran a finger down her spine, and she shuddered.

"Maybe I'm afraid you'll want more." She stared at a picture on the shelf. It all had something to do with Karen, but she hadn't had time to work it out. Karen had believed in her. Karen had died.

"Setting the limits again, Jennie?" His voice was colder, wafting over her like a draft on her bare skin. "I can have you, but I can't make any claims on you—is that it?"

Cursing, he bounded out of bed and stalked to the washer before the buzzer could sound again. He tossed his clothes in the drier and set it with a vicious twist of his wrist. "Maybe this is all *you* wanted."

Jennie nodded dumbly. Where had the hollow feeling in her chest come from? She'd felt the same way the time she fell off Glaze and got all the wind knocked out of her—and when she'd heard about Karen.

"Tell me what's standing between us, Jennie. I'm getting tired of guessing."

She sat up, hugging her knees to her chest. Being attacked for trying to protect him, knowing she was only hurting him, made her irritable. She was upset with the clumsy way she was handling the situation. Couldn't he see it was for his own good? She was trying to remove the stardust from his eyes. "You have to guess, don't you? You know almost nothing about me, about my life before I came here, or even why I came here. Unless, of course, you've heard stories in town."

He had heard the stories, but he wanted to go back farther into her past. What *did* he really know about her? he wondered. "Why did you get into music?"

Startled, she answered as honestly as she could, "To reach people. To tell them what I knew, saw, felt. Maybe help them with what they were going through."

"Did you accomplish any of that?"

"Sometimes. A few of the fan letters I received said so. I turned out a handful of good albums."

"Then why did you quit?"

She looked at him unblinkingly, her answer succinct. "Personal failures."

Jake thought for a minute. She hadn't told him much, but she'd been honest, chillingly so. He didn't think she ever lied. She kept a lot to herself, but she didn't lie. That worried him. There were some things a man liked to hear whether they were true or not. It wouldn't be easy living without hearing them. Did she ever make things easy on herself? He doubted it. "I imagine it would be hard to have a relationship on the road, to meet someone."

"They manage to seek you out."

"Hard to keep a relationship going, then."

"Yeah." She stared at the shelf for a few minutes, and the silence stretched between them. Finally she said, "The men are nice."

"Are they?" It made his skin crawl to ask.

Keenly aware of the nuances in his voice, she glanced up at him, then laughed at the scowl on his face. It was a lilting, melody-filled laugh that Jake suddenly longed to hear again even as he rebelled against it.

"*Your* men are nice," she amended with a grin. "I liked them."

"Oh. I thought we were still on the road."

"I got off that topic a long time ago."

"Last night you couldn't put distance or anger between us, so you put people there. I saw through your scheme."

"I know. I'm sorry. I wanted to be alone." She laughed, this time mockingly. "It sounds melodramatic, but it's true."

"Why?"

She made a face. "You're awfully inquisitive today."

"I want to know you better—before we make love again."

She held herself utterly still. He was standing beside the bed, towering over her with his nearness. He touched her cheek with the back of his hand. She pulled the sheet up to her breasts. Sometimes he could make her feel so naked, so vulnerable.

A flicker of contempt for the sheet flashed in his eyes. It wasn't as if he hadn't seen all of her, she thought.

"You'll find anything to keep between us, won't you? Damnedest part is, I let you do it." With sudden force he jerked the sheet away. "Not anymore, Jennie. I want to hear it all. I want to get close to you in every way."

She ran a hand through her hair, gathering it from where it stuck to her neck. Hot air prickled over the moisture on her skin. "Where do you want me to start? With the drugs? The orgies?"

"How about the girl you were living with?"

She swallowed but found the courage to look him in the eye. "Did the sheriff tell you about her?"

A smile twisted his face. "You don't think for a minute I believe you're a lesbian."

"Some people in town think so."

"I don't live in town."

"I'll hurt you, Jake."

"You do it every time you turn your back on me. I don't like it, but I can take it."

She shook her head, despairing of ever making this man understand she was a dangerous woman to love. "Jake, please."

"What was her name?"

"Karen."

He listened, running one hand down her face in a comforting stroke. It wasn't sexual, but oh, how she wished . . . If they could only make love again—potent, soul-shattering love—it would wipe out all the hurt. But some things had to be faced, including the past. She took a deep breath. "That's her picture, in the blue frame there."

He got it off the shelf, studied it for a moment, then handed it to her. "Who was she?"

As much as she despised the word, Jennie used the only one that fit. "A groupie. She wanted to write songs. She had so many dreams and no idea where to begin. She got on the bus one day by sleeping with one of the crew and stayed for the rest of the tour. I wanted to help her."

"Why?"

"Because she needed me. Because she believed in me so much."

"Did you?"

"I was tired of reaching out to a mass of faces, writing songs that were nothing more than light entertainment. I wanted to really help somebody."

"What's wrong with that?"

"I believed my own press clippings, don't you see? I thought I could get up there on stage and explain love to people, for heaven's sake!" She ran her hands through her hair again until it was thoroughly mussed and tangled. Then she counted her faults on her fingers. "I was naïve enough to think I could help a mixed-up teenage runaway get over drugs, develop self-esteem, and even start publishing songs, if only we could go away someplace quiet like the ranch. Talk about egotistical." The sentence ended with a sigh. Jennie rubbed her eyes. "I can't help the world; I couldn't even help one person."

"And it's your fault?"

She ran her fingers down the edge of the picture frame. "For some reason, ever since you came I've been thinking about her. She believed in me and I failed her, Jake. I don't want that kind of blind adoration from anyone."

"Or that kind of clinging."

"You make it sound selfish, but—" The drier buzzed before she could say, "I love you and I don't want you hurt."

"Why don't you take a shower? You'll feel cooler," he said.

He ran a hand over her hair, and she kissed his palm, holding it to her lips for one brief moment. "Don't you see you shouldn't believe in me?"

"I love you," he said, without qualifying the statement, with no hedging, with no doubts.

But wasn't his loving the great and talented Jennie Cisco, not seeing the vulnerable and human and temperamental woman inside, the heart of the problem?

He held her cheek in his hand. "I want more than a few days in bed with you."

She shut her eyes tightly, refusing to fish for a commitment of any kind. "Realistically, it's all we may have. Three or four days. However long you stay."

"I won't settle for that, Jennie. I want more."

"Don't, Jake. All my life I've been tugged and pushed, and have had managers and promoters and producers making demands on me." It wasn't coming out the way she meant it. She sighed in exasperation and started again. "I realize you're a man who gives orders—"

"No, Jennie. We make our own rules. Us. Not you setting the limits, not me giving orders. It's us now. Didn't you feel something when we made love?"

Yes, she'd felt it—a flood of emotions she couldn't deal with. He was showing her how to live again. And like being a newborn, it was frightening and painful. "Just let me think, Jake. I need time and space."

She was up and halfway to the bathroom when he caught her roughly by the shoulders.

"You're running away again."

She looked at him bleakly. Until she was sure her love wouldn't hurt him somehow, she had to have the courage to let him go, even if he didn't understand.

He didn't. All the hope drained out of him. He'd been a fool to think he could make her love him simply by making love. Just because a man loved a woman didn't mean he could make her change her mind. Lord, hadn't he learned that lesson we. enough? He let her go, his hands falling to his sides. "I'll be at the computer, entering some data. Can I use your phone first?"

"Sure," she said hollowly.

She locked the bathroom door and leaned her forehead against the cold mirror. "Great move, kid. Why didn't you just pop him one and scream rape? What a way to say thanks for the memories."

It had been wonderful, and she'd stolen it from him and herself by pushing him away. His sin? He wanted to get close. Did she have to take it out on him, because she was afraid for both of them?

She stood in the shower, arms tight to her sides.

hands in fists, wishing the water wouldn't wash the feel, the smell of him away.

"Yeah, honey. I should be able to stop by in a couple weeks, maybe three. You know I can't make promises. . . . You betcha, sweetheart. Anywhere you say. You pick the best restaurant in Pocatello, and I'll treat you to it. . . . Fat? Never. I love you just as you are."

Jennie stood at the foot of the stairs, the pain cutting into her like barbed wire. Her hair was wet and rebraided, the tip dripping on one breast like a leaky faucet. Inside she felt like cracked porcelain held together with glue and willpower. But what hurt most was losing the handful of memories. They'd been tarnished, stolen.

Jake looked up from where he was perched on the arm of the sofa and winked, beckoning her with one hand. Too shocked to object, she stepped beside him and felt his hand run up her thigh—not sensuously, proprietarily. She stepped back fast, but he grasped her hand, kneading it softly.

"Sure, you can sleep over," he said. "Have a bag packed, and I'll call when I get there. See you later, honey. Love you too." He hung up.

"You'd better have an explanation for that," she said in a flat, steel-edged voice. "Well?"

The realization dawned on him that the flush on her cheeks wasn't from their lovemaking. He grinned, then laughed outright.

Jennie was practically shaking from the emotions seething inside her. "You think it's funny? Setting up dates on my phone? Or were you trying to make me jealous? Well, you just bought yourself a ticket out of here."

"Jennie—" he began soothingly. "Her name's Shauna. She's blond, petite, and the best thing that ever happened in my life. Until now. And I plan to hold onto her until another man takes her away. Ten or fifteen years from now."

"How very calculating of you."

"A father can't keep his daughter forever. And a pretty one like Shauna is bound to be snapped up."

"Daughter?"

"Seven years old."

"You never mentioned one."

"It's hard."

"To say, 'I'm divorced and I have a daughter'?"

"To say, 'She lives with her mother and I see her two, maybe three times a year,' yes."

Jennie watched a flash of pain flicker across his face before he squelched it.

He toyed with the afghan on the back of the sofa. "Okay, I owe you one. Come here." Taking her hand and leading her upstairs, he retrieved his wallet from the nightstand. "Hope you don't mind." He was almost sheepish, sitting on the edge of the bed, unfolding ten different photos of his little girl. He explained exactly when and where each was taken, sparing a few words for the ones that had been taken without him and sent on by his ex-wife and her new husband.

Jennie listened, caught up in the anecdotes that accompanied each picture. Mostly she watched his crinkled smile, the wry twist of his lips, and the occassional pain he couldn't minimize with a grimace or a shrug.

"Did your ex give you a rough time?" she asked softly.

He realized honesty worked both ways, and it hurt deeply. "She fell in love with someone else."

"You let her go?"

"I begged her to come back. Literally."

Jennie didn't have to guess what an admission like his would cost a man.

"She came back," he said, lying back on the bed, one arm crooked under his head. "We gave it another try. I failed that inspection also. It would have been easier if she'd packed, written a note, and simply left. It was the back-and-forth part that killed me, never knowing from one day to the next if she was going to stay or go to the other man." He shrugged. There didn't seem to be any other way to sum up the rotten twists of fate. "When she married him they got custody of Shauna. A more stable home environment, the judge said. I travel too much." He carefully refolded the pictures.

"Why didn't you fight?"

"The fact is, my life isn't stable enough. Not for a child *or* a wife, it appears." He glanced at her quickly, then back at the ceiling. "I'm more settled now. My computer work could keep me in an office practically year-round if I wanted."

She didn't catch the hint. She was still thinking about his little girl and how much she meant to her father. "So you see her a few times a year. Shauna."

"She's bigger every time I see her. I call when there's an accident I think she'll hear about on TV. I always let her know I'm all right."

"But if you did settle down, wouldn't you try to get her back?"

"Stop pressing, Jennie. There are some things it's easier to give up than lose. I'm not proud of my decision, but I'm sticking to it. I make my payments, send cards, and keep in touch. We gave her enough grief when her mother and I were together. She needs the family she's got now."

Everything in Jennie told her to argue with him, but it wasn't the time. She lay down beside him on the coverlet, both of them lost in their own thoughts.

"That was long distance. I'll pay you for the call."

"Don't be ridiculous." Her voice was choked, and she wiped the tears from the corners of her eyes. He wouldn't accept pity any more than she would. "Thank you for telling me."

"There's something else. What I bought in town, I'm sorry I forgot to use them."

"Don't worry."

"You said that last night. Jennie, I could never walk away from another child."

She smiled wryly. "I'm on the Pill, Jake."

"Why didn't you say so?"

"I didn't want to yell it out the door as you were driving away."

He laughed with her, but he was a little confused. "You live like a recluse in the mountains and you need those?"

"They regulate my cycle. My manager thought it would be better career-wise if I didn't have 'off days,' and mine were definitely off. Just because I'm semiretired doesn't mean I want to feel miserable every month."

"That bad, huh?"

"Ever try canceling a concert because of cramps?"

"My ex said having a baby helped her."

"Gee, thanks. I'll get one next time I'm in town."

"Try the all-night drugstore."

They laughed together, and Jennie thought how good it felt. Then his hand pressed softly on her stomach.

"I wouldn't mind giving you a baby."

"Talk about dependency!" she wailed playfully. "Some poor little innocent babe depending on me for a normal life? Ha!"

"You'd be a beautiful mother. Why do you put yourself down?"

"To keep the old ego in check. Otherwise I start thinking I'm earth mother to the world, out to save every wayward soul through my music. My art."

"Jennie."

"Don't lecture me, Jake. Let's try to be happy for now."

"You've got every right to be angry with me. I can't say two words about Shauna without choking up, but I insist you drag up all the pain in your past."

She touched his face. Talking about Karen had helped. "I still don't have my life all in order, but I want to lay to rest the part with Karen. Give me a little more time."

Time. The morning was flying by, and he'd have to be at the fire line in an hour. There were data he needed and information he had to pull. But there was Jennie, next to him on the bed, and he thought of how little time they had to be together.

He unbuttoned her blouse, absently playing with the end of her braid, brushing it over her nipples until they peaked. "Once more," he said quietly, and she nodded.

It was the only communication they needed. Clothes were removed, sheets pushed aside, oppressive heat ignored, then doubled by their bodies. She was on top of him, taunting his chest with love bites, when he dug his fingers into her lean flanks. It took only a movement, the barest hint that he wanted to be inside her, and she was ready for him.

They fit so well together, felt so right. She tightened around him, and he wanted to roll her under him and let his passion explode right then, but it was her turn, he decided. He wanted her to have the same nerve-scalding release he was fighting to hold back. If they didn't reach the dual ecstasy men and women dreamed of, at least he'd see that she was fulfilled. But maybe, if he timed it just right . . .

Jennie arched and took him deeper, rocking as she clutched her thighs to his sides, calling his name, entreating him mindlessly, arousing him almost beyond endurance. He watched her move, the shadows of pleasure, frustration, and mounting passion racing across her face. She was magnificent. A wanton, breathless smile curved her kiss-swollen lips. Her breasts were small, firm, and peaked, rising and falling with her rapid, impatient breaths.

He dragged her mouth down to his. He wanted one more kiss before she went utterly wild and the pulsing of her sweet core made him give in to his own rhythmic explosion. If they never made love again, this would be their one perfect time, the one they shared.

Afterward, Jake smiled to himself, gently dabbing the sweat off her back with a corner of the sheet. A knock on the door made them both jump.

Her eyes flew open.

His eyes darkened. He had no intention of moving. "Now, Jennie," he whispered, an impudent smile of his face.

Someone's feet shuffled on the porch.

"It could be important," she whispered.

"So could this." He moved a little inside her, and her eyes fluttered shut. But she was right—it could concern the fire, he realized, although he wasn't about to let her have the last word. He kissed her thoroughly, ravishingly.

She swept on a dressing gown and leaned around the screen that blocked the loft from the living room. The man on the porch had given up and gone. She sighed and sat on the edge of the bed watching

Jake, his pants already on, reaching for his cowboy boots.

Just my luck to love a cowboy, she thought. She blinked in mild surprise, trying to rewrite the lyric even though it was perfect as it stood. Half of the melody played in her head already. She should get out her Dobro and run through a few chords; get it on tape before she lost it.

But she was too busy staring at Jake, the muscles of his back in motion as he bent to tug on another boot. She noticed several small horizontal scratches on his back. Were they from branches? Underbrush? Her fingernails?

He caught her eye. Stopping in front of her, shrugging into his shirt, he lifted the brushy tip of her braid and kissed it. She buttoned the shirt for him, freeing his hands to slide inside her gown and touch her breasts.

He didn't kiss her, although he inclined his head to. "See you tonight," he said, and he was gone.

A man of few words. Macho. Tender. A cowboy. Did she really love him? Yes. *Just my luck.* She really ought to write that down, she thought.

If only they could keep their relationship as simple as a good song, they might stand half a chance.

Nine

It was a good song. Jennie worked on the chorus and charted the main chords before lunch. Trucks came to the ranch and left. When a plane flew low overhead, she looked up briefly. It was a bomber, probably filled with water or flame retardant, she thought. Then she went back to work. She could have been in the heart of New York and not been bothered by the noise, her concentration was so intense. Before dusk, Jake dropped by and ran through some data on his computer. A quick kiss good-bye was followed by a much longer one, leaving them both reluctant to part, until a shout and the arrival of a new crew of firemen drew Jake outside.

They were setting up some sort of tent beside the bunkhouses, but Jennie was too busy to care. For the first time she had a glimmer of hope concerning the two of them. She didn't know how they'd work it out or what arrangement they would come to, and she was keenly aware he'd made no promises. But where there was love there was hope.

Another good lyric, she thought. She should write it down. First she had to record the demo for "Just My Luck."

She tuned her guitar, set up the tape deck and microphone, and pushed the play/record buttons. There was no tape in the machine. In fact, a quick search told her she was completely out of blank tapes. She muttered a few halfhearted curses, scrounged in the built-in cabinets beside the fireplace, and found a pile of old tapes she could record over.

Jake came back that night—and the next. Jennie was surprised every time she woke and he was there beside her. She was surprised how easily he'd become part of her life, amazed how full her life had become, how rich their lovemaking was, how increasingly tender.

The ranch was the bustling center of a growing number of fire fighters. There was a constant hum of voices and trucks, and the sound of an occasional helicopter landing on the flattest part of the valley. Tents, Porta-Johns, and Jeeps dotted the land. Firemen freed up from other fires were joining to fight this one. If she hadn't been able to help people in the past, at least she was doing so now, by sharing her ranch.

She and Jake didn't talk about the fire. It was extinguished in places, burning in dozens of small patches and one large area; each spot needed attention, each threatening to explode into a major inferno with the slightest provocation. All areas of the fire had to be seen to by crews; coordination and prediction were paramount. Jake was kept busy, but never too busy to come by.

In those stolen hours he asked about her career,

her past. Wanting to know everything but more interested in how she felt than what she did. They shared mundane things—likes and dislikes, favorite foods and favorite places, private jokes and public good-byes.

"I suppose you expect me to cook you another breakfast," she said halfheartedly. He'd left her bed only two hours earlier to direct his crew and reconnoiter with a meteorologist.

He came up behind her at the stove, wrapping his big arms around her and giving her a more-than-brotherly squeeze. "I'm getting used to having the little woman do my cooking. Uh!" An elbow in his midsection stopped his teasing.

"I'll cook your breakfast, all right."

"Yeah, and fry my eggs, burn my toast, and settle my hash while your at it. All the while never working up a sweat."

"I only work up a sweat—"

"—in bed," he said for her.

Jennie turned a shade of pink like fireplace embers breathed back to life. Jake didn't miss her reaction. Remembering a few smoldering nights with Jennie, he felt a little flushed himself.

In a matter of minutes she'd set a plate of food in front of him, abruptly pulling out a chair so his elevated feet hit the floor. She sat down primly, and they dug in.

"You had a big pow-wow with those computer people camping by the trees."

"Comparing programs."

"And?"

"Mine's better."

Jennie sighed and rolled her eyes. "The male ego! There was a question I wanted to ask you."

"Ask away." He sopped up some eggs with his toast.

"How is it they can run their computer from a tent, when you require my kitchen table?"

Jake thought he did a good job at hiding his smile on such short notice. Formulating a reply took a little longer. "Uh, mmm." He filled his mouth with a heaping forkful of food and took a minute to chew. "They brought a generator."

"And in a week you haven't been able to get one up here?"

"You want to try and kick me out?"

The challenge was uttered with a swagger that was definitely becoming. For a moment Jennie pictured the ensuing wrestling match on the kitchen floor. But they both had work to get to, she realized. "The big question is, can any of your hotshot computers predict where the fire's going?"

"Only He can do that." Jake pointed his fork in the air before spearing another sausage. He set down the utensil to run his fingers over her cheek, sliding a strand of hair behind her ear. She was wearing her hair loose, showing the wild Jennie only he saw. She'd braid it up before going outside, but for now he wanted her to know he appreciated the gesture.

Talk about male ego, he thought. She sure knew how to build his up. He'd possessed her as much as any man could possess a wild thing, and it made him so damn proud, he wanted her to be his forever. But lingering concern haunted her eyes. "Don't worry, Jennie. We're doing everything—"

"I know."

At least he got a smile out of her, a grudging, forced one. They ate in silence for a few minutes.

"You've been writing songs," he said.

A week ago his statement would have led to fireworks between them. Now she looked mildly surprised. "You've been eavesdropping again."

"One of the men mentioned a song you keep playing."

"I do that when I'm working."

The request "Can I hear it?" was almost out of his mouth when he reminded himself Jennie was still a private woman. She'd play it for him when she was ready. However, his curiosity wasn't satisfied. "What's it called?"

" 'Just My Luck to Love a Cowboy.' "

For a moment, watching the twinkle in her eyes, he didn't know if it was a title or a taunt. He guessed both, and he fastened his gaze on his plate as the possibilities hit him. She wasn't being coy. If anything, Jennie was too direct. Jake's throat was tight. "Do you mean that?"

She nodded, her brown eyes somber.

He linked his fingers with hers, and she twined them, palms pressed together. "Are you going to sell it to somebody else to sing?"

Jennie looked off into the distance. She was half smiling, her mind miles away. Jake was struck with the thought that he could spend a lifetime with this woman, and she'd still be a mystery to him. "I don't know. Nobody else could sing it the way I could."

He laughed, tossing his napkin on the table. Bending to kiss her good-bye, he whispered in her ear, "Talk about ego."

Patience. Humor. Teasing. Making love. Jake considered every angle. You didn't push someone like Jennie; she was too proud, too strong. She'd fight back. He'd have to wait for each crack in the facade.

If they had more time it might work. Every day he'd be able to stop by, showing her by steady attention that need and dependency weren't the same. He looked into the hills, the plume of grayish black churning in the distance, and knew time was something they didn't have. There was no time to build trust.

Would his job be a problem? The near-constant travel had been a monkey wrench in his marriage. The danger was always there, too. Was Jennie afraid for him? "Don't need me—I might not be there," she had said. Didn't it work both ways? If she started needing him, one bad gust of wind could see to it he wouldn't be there for her either.

The dangerous part of his job wasn't something he liked to dwell on. Except for the brief period after his divorce when he hadn't cared how many risks he took, he was a careful, responsible man. Why had he thrown caution to the winds where Jennie was concerned? It was too late to change things, he realized. Like the danger, he merely accepted it. She was a part of him, and he'd do everything he could to keep her.

He dusted off the seat of his jeans, passed on his canteen to another fire fighter, and got back to work. Walking up the steep incline toward the row of men, he remembered the passion he and Jennie had shared and the frail lines of trust they'd built. They were almost as frail as this line of people and their shovels, trying to stop a raging inferno, he thought.

He pulled his bandanna up over his nose, noticed Burt was slowing down, and told him to take a break. Then he dug another shovelful of dirt. Time was growing short, and he couldn't press Jennie for any kind of commitment. But if he couldn't bind her to him somehow, the fire that blazed when they touched might be nothing but ashes when the fire in the hills had burned itself out.

• • •

She'd finished another song. Three in two days—quite a pace, she thought. Ideas had been popping up from all sides, inspiration flowing like a cresting river. Turning out songs for others had become a job, and not a joy. The songs she'd been writing over the past few days were for her, and they just kept coming.

But her latest attempt wasn't going well. There were chord changes that didn't come easy, and rough transitions. Above all, the melody sounded so familiar, she didn't know where to take it, and found herself frustrated because nothing she did sounded right. It was already in her head; she just couldn't pin it down.

She worked until suppertime. Deciding to get at least some of the song on tape, she played back the last song she'd recorded. As it ended, she was lost in thought and forgot to hit the pause button. A series of chords began, and it suddenly dawned on Jennie where she'd gotten her new melody. It was the next song on the old tape she'd been recording over, and she'd unconsciously picked it up. She kept listening.

It wasn't one of hers. The voice was unsteady, young. It was Karen's voice.

Jennie rewound the tape and listened, then rewound it again. She couldn't see past the tears, and feared she'd press the wrong button and erase it. Over and over, she listened to Karen's voice, Karen's lyrics.

He didn't knock. The sound of her singing stopped him halfway up the porch steps. Her voice was different, thinner, tentative, as if she didn't know the song well. Jake opened the screen and slowly walked inside.

She was sitting on the floor in front of the fireplace, sheets of music scattered around her, cradling a guitar. The melody was tinny and had a country feel to it, and the voice kept cracking. Tears streamed down her face.

Immediately bending down on one knee, he rocked her in his arms. "Baby, what's wrong?"

She sobbed into his shoulder, shaking her head, pressing her face against him. He was so good to her, expressing a tenderness she didn't deserve. She tried to pull out of his arms.

"Listen." She played the song on the recorder.

He crouched in front of her, listening, wiping her puffy face with his thumbs. It didn't take him long to figure it out. "That's Karen, isn't it?"

She nodded, then swung the guitar between them, fumbling with the chords. "I've got to learn it."

"Why?"

"So I can send it to the recording company, that's why. I never did."

He sat down heavily beside her. "You want to tell me about it?"

She hugged her guitar, and pain furrowed her brows. "She was doing so well that summer, off drugs. She took responsibility for her horse, her room, her chores. We painted the whole corral fence; it hasn't been done since. She worked on her songs while I worked on mine. And she was *good*, Jake, talented. The songs were good."

He nodded, because Jennie needed him to believe her.

"I'd signed her up for high school in the fall, down in Lone Pine. I never should have—she was still troubled, but I didn't see it."

"What happened?"

"Didn't the sheriff tell you?" There was bitterness in her voice.

"What's he got to do with it?"

"Oh damn." She tossed a guitar pick across the

room and wiped her tears with the back of her hand. "I thought Karen was improving, but she only acted that way to win my acceptance. That was all she ever wanted, from anyone. Back in school again she needed friends to accept her, so she bragged about her life in the rock-and-roll business, the famous people she knew, the stars she'd slept with. When that didn't go over, she fell in with a crowd who would accept her. To them she bragged about the drugs she'd taken.

"She was writing fewer songs, doing fewer chores. I thought she was busy with homework and let it slide a little, but it was a sign. Then homecoming came up, and she begged to go to the dance. She ended up at a party. It was raided. Drugs were found. All her so-called friends blamed her. It was easy to point a finger—she was the outsider. As if no one in Lone Pine had heard of drugs until Karen came here.

"Anyway, Sheriff Kechnie released her into my custody. Karen was hysterical. She ran away that night. A month later they found her in L.A. The sheriff called me and offered to drive me down to identify her. I thought she was in a lineup, in trouble again. She was in the morgue, an OD victim."

Jennie's voice wound down like a stereo whose plug had been pulled. Telling Jake had taken something out of her. She didn't cry anymore, just stared at the dust clouds stirring up outside. Jake stroked her back and held her, thinking how badly she must have been hurt to go from being so eager to help people, to stopping giving altogether—to turn her back on the world, keeping it at bay with a shotgun. "You tried to help."

"I was so naïve."

"Jennie, you did more for her than anyone, even

her parents. Where were they? No one else so much as tried."

"Yes." For the first time, in the strong circle of his arms, she let herself believe she'd done her best with Karen. "But maybe I was so wrapped up in trying to mold her into a better person that I wasn't listening when she needed me most."

"And maybe she didn't want you to help her."

"I should have read the signs."

He shook her gently. "Since when are you obliged to read minds?"

She knew it was true. She let thoughts come to her she'd never allowed herself to consider; that part of the fault was Karen's. Jennie had made communication between them as open as possible, but there were times Karen had chosen to close it off, to have secrets. Jennie might be able to forgive herself, she realized. The hard part would be forgiving Karen for throwing her young life away. Just admitting she blamed Karen in any way hurt. "A lot of it was there in her songs. The need for acceptance. The pain."

"You listened."

Jennie hung her head. "I analyzed the songs to see if they were marketable."

"Are they?"

"Some are." Her hand strayed over the scattered sheets of music. "I really like this one."

"Why don't you record it?"

"So I can forgive myself? Forgive her? So many easy things you want, Mr. Kramer. Anything else?"

He looked away, a shaft of pain in his eyes. It might not have been the right time, but he couldn't risk missing the chance. "Selfish as it may sound, I want you to love me, Jennie. I want that more than anything."

She looked at him for a moment. His jaw was

clenched, his lips set tight. How hard it must have been for him to say those words, she realized. But then, she'd never made it easy for him.

"That's a simple one." She turned his face to hers with her fingertips. Her fingers were still thrumming with the feel of the guitar strings. His cheek was shaved and smooth. She wondered if she'd ever get tired of touching him, and knew in the brief time they'd have together she'd never be able to touch him enough. "You're another person I could fail."

"I'm a man, Jennie, not a mixed-up teenager. It's my responsibility to tell you what I need. If you can't give it, I'll just have to live without it. I don't expect you to save my life. Hell, lady, I'm here to save yours."

Holding her close hadn't left him unmoved. He could be gentle and supportive when it was called for, but her body against his was like a firebrand, and no matter how selfish the motive, he had to touch her.

"Shh," he whispered, promising himself he'd stop with each of her soft-falling tears. But her hair was so soft to his kiss, her skin so like hot satin. Her shoulders shook and trembled, and he wrapped his arms around them. And when her mouth begged his tongue inside, he lost all sense of restraint and reached for the spot that made her come alive.

The floor was bare wood. Bare skin soon met it. Their mouths wouldn't be separated, but clothes had to be shed, zippers unzipped, buttons undone by fumbling fingers. He wiped her hair off her face and kissed her once, completely, poised to enter her, until her words stopped him.

"Why, Jake, why?" Tears welled in her brown eyes. "Why do you love me so much?"

"I can show you better than I can tell you." His

eyes were stormy, his face taut. He pressed inside her then, and watched a tear roll back into her hair. He slid out, then in, slick, sweet, and slow. Her tears tore him up, but she needed him, she needed this. He was taking her away from the pain, murmuring with every thrust, "I love you, Jennie, love you. Let it go, baby, just let it go."

She knew she should be embarrassed, having fallen apart. But he accepted it. Her body trembled with sobs, too overcome to do anything in response to his movements. He accepted that, too, and gradually her self-consciousness melted away. She forgot everything but the feel of him inside her. Luxuriating in the growing heat, sinking in the molten sea as Jake's voice called to her, *Let it go, let go.*

Then she was moving with him. A crescendo built so fast after their unhurried beginning that it made her gasp, waves reverberating through her like the quivering tones of a tuning fork, struck once, and then again.

He barely moved, barely thrust, feeling the amazing ripples of ecstasy fluttering inside her, drawing him so swiftly to the edge, he shuddered and exploded until he thought it would never end. Dazed by the experience, he was convinced he'd never loved a woman more.

They shared a quick shower to wash the tears away at last, then a long good-bye kiss. He told her he loved her, and she clung to him, whispering his name, choking on the words she couldn't say—apologies for the rough times, promises and questions. He loved her, but would he stay? Could a love that had blossomed in a matter of nights survive the days to come? How close was the fire now? Would he stay?

"Wait," she cried as he stepped off the veranda.

He'd come there for a reason: He had something

important to tell her. He'd never said it. He turned at the sound of her voice and knew he couldn't say it now. Their time was almost up.

A look passed between them that neither understood. It was as if they were saying a final good-bye. As if this were the last time they'd be close. As if something had ended, but neither knew what came next.

Then it faded, and Jennie realized she wasn't ready to ask him for promises. That night she'd wake and find him beside her. Maybe in the dark her pride would let her bend a little and ask him to stay.

Maybe.

But that night he didn't come back.

Men were milling about in the kitchen when Jennie came down the next morning. Jake's had been the first voice she'd heard. He glanced up briefly but left it to her to say hello to the men gathered around his computer screen. She nodded and made small talk, graciously smiling at a comment about her last record.

Jake said nothing, and the men's attention quickly returned to the screen. He was keeping his distance, and she sensed it immediately. He was busy, yes, but that wasn't the reason.

When he'd walked off her veranda the previous day and she'd called to him, had she acted too desperate? Too clinging? Had she repelled him by showing such naked need? She was being paranoid, and she knew it. It wasn't like her to design overwrought scenarios of rejection. He'd stared at her with as much longing as she'd shown him. But he was distant now, preoccupied. No matter how she tried to talk herself out of it, the feeling persisted.

Jake jammed the keys and saw a line of conso-nants repeat themselves across the screen. He cursed and backspaced, trying to keep his mind on the machine. He'd noticed the dark circles beneath Jen-nie's eyes the minute she walked in, and they'd made him feel like hell. She'd had a hard night after dragging herself through those memories. He'd been there for a few tears, but not through the dark hours of the night. He wanted to hold Jennie, to comfort her, to share a few words of support with her, but he couldn't with all the men around. As a result, he felt like a heel.

He was also guilty as sin. He'd known the day before what was drawing everyone to the ranch, had seen the way the wind was whipping the fire straight toward *El Dobro.* He'd come back to warn her; it could be a matter of a day, maybe two. She should be ready to leave. But he hadn't warned her, and his excuses for keeping it from her were beginning to wear thin.

If only they could talk privately, Jennie thought. She wanted to tell him she was better. She'd worked out a lot of things during the night, and had awak-ened feeling much freer from the past, ready to start over—with him. But Jake hadn't been there. Now she had the feeling he didn't want to be in the same room with her. "Am I interrupting?" she asked no one in particular.

A broad-shouldered ranger in a Smokey-the-Bear hat answered jovially, "This is your home, Miss Cisco. I'm sorry if *we're* disturbing *you.*"

"No bother." Jake glanced up and quickly looked away. Jennie'd thought that remark would get him. It certainly hadn't been her attitude when *he'd* ar-rived. "The only thing that bothers me, gentlemen, is the fire. How's it going?"

Jake punched the computer keys and muttered a few terse words. One look at his hard-set face, and she knew it was bad. "Jake?"

A ranger named Mike spoke first. "The proverbial good news, bad news, I'm afraid. A storm is blowing in off the Pacific. Looks like it'll douse these fires."

"That's good, isn't it?"

"Not entirely," Mike said, after waiting in vain for some comment from Jake.

"The bad news, then?"

"Storms bring rain, that's true. However, they also bring heat lightning and more wind."

"But the rain will put out any fires the lightning starts."

"But the wind comes first as it blows the storm in—"

"Pushing the fire before it," Jake cut in, his voice uncharacteristically harsh. "We could lose another ten thousand acres. A few hours of steady wind could spread this thing everywhere. It's a project fire now. We'll require all the manpower available."

The screen door slammed and another man joined them, carrying a lap-top computer. "Let's compare the data so far," he said, without introduction.

"Set it down here." Jake was curt, fast, and professional, fiercely intent on the amber screen. He was getting ready for battle.

While they fed diskettes into the second machine, Jennie served them all lemonade. A look passed between her and Jake when she handed him his glass. He took a long sip and handed it back to her. She drank from the same glass, only fleetingly aware that their little ritual had caused a lag in the conversation.

The room was becoming stuffy.

"Well, gentlemen, I will do what I rarely do, and leave the real work to the menfolk."

They chuckled. She smiled as best she could. "The kitchen is all yours, but the ranch is mine. I'd appreciate it if you kept this little old fire at bay. I've got some extra buckets if you need them."

Their companionable laughter as she exited couldn't stop the fear curdling in her stomach. Rain was coming, but her ranch could be destroyed before it arrived. From the veranda she looked out over a pasture crawling with men, women, equipment, and trucks—even a helicopter. Why would they erect a camp there if the fire was coming this way? They wouldn't, she thought. Allowing her place to be used as a base was probably the best thing she could have done to save it.

And, of course, she'd met Jake. She loved him, and the more she saw of him, the more she admired him. He was completely capable. Everyone waited for his command. He was brave without being foolhardy, organized but not dogmatic. He took suggestions in stride but gave orders without hesitation. His crew respected his opinion because he respected theirs. But could one man stop a rushing fire swept on by the wind? Thinking of the danger he faced caused a sense of dread to snake up her skin, and she shivered in the stifling heat.

He'd been distant to her. And although she knew it was silly to worry, that he was busy and distracted, she couldn't shake the feeling that an icy finger was tapping on her shoulder. She'd gotten just a taste of what she'd feel when the fire was over and he was gone. How could memories ever be enough?

Ten

"I told you before, Jake, I won't be an evacuee." She didn't like orders; he should have known that by now. She stood beside the piano, crossing her arms defiantly.

It was barely eleven o'clock. Jake had left three hours earlier and taken a chopper around the fire's perimeter. It was worse, on a direct path down Cerro Gordo toward the ranch. He ran a hand roughly through his hair. "We're doing what we can—"

"So you keep saying. I want to help too. I want to stay."

"No. We've got all the people we could call up."

"But it's my ranch."

"There's nothing you can do."

"Except sit in some hotel room and wait to hear whether you're okay." She hugged away the shiver, but couldn't suppress the icy crystalizing of her spine. What if no one called her? She wasn't his next of kin. If something happened to him she'd hear it on the evening news.

"I can't leave, Jake." She tried to come up with

other reasons, other excuses. She waved her hand at the room. "This is my home. Do you know how many years I worked, how many tours I had to do, to get this?"

"So it's the ranch."

"It's you, Jake," she said quietly. But time was short, and she had to fit in all she had to say, even if the timing was wrong. She'd imagined the moment so many other ways. "I love you," she said. "I want to stay because I couldn't bear to wait while you're out there in danger."

He flinched and turned away. He had no argument with her reasons. He'd heard it from Shauna, from his ex-wife. Hearing it from Jennie hurt twice as much. Would he lose everyone he loved because of a job? Because he felt honor-bound to do all he could? "I can't promise I'll be safe. I'd be lying if I said nothing ever went wrong."

He looked so tired, she had to touch him. Then they held each other tightly, as if wanting to hold time itself.

"Say it again, Jennie." He kissed the top of her hair softly.

"Don't make me go."

Her plea cut into him, and he closed his eyes. They swayed to silent music. "The part about loving me."

"Forever and ever."

He listened. He held on. He took a deep breath. "I love you too. That's why I have to get you out of here."

The sudden irony of it all made her laugh. "But I love you, and that's why I don't want to go."

"Think of the ranch, Jennie. Here, look." He gently turned her, his large hands heavy on her shoulders. "Your piano, your rugs, your music books."

"I can buy another piano. Other rugs." She couldn't

talk to her possessions, sing to them, or hold them against her heart as she sighed. The long look he'd given her on the veranda suddenly made sense. "You knew about this yesterday, didn't you? That's why you came here."

"There was no sense worrying you, as long as we had a handle on it." He searched for another angle. "I warned you the first time we met that you might have to evacuate."

"The old 'I told you so' defense. I believe my answer was no then too."

"Okay," he said, "so I let it ride. I didn't want to give you time to carve your arguments in stone. You're a damn stubborn woman."

"I'm a fighter, Jake. I can't stand aside and watch this place destroyed. And I can't go into town and just wait for news—about the ranch, about you—"

Her voice broke, and she turned her back on him until she had herself under control. She was too close to falling apart, to flinging herself in his arms and begging him not to do what he had to, what he'd come there for in the first place. She touched the piano keys, played a few trills, a run, then made a discordant bang as her fist came down. "Everything we do is at cross-purposes. I want to stay, you want me to go. You want to save my ranch, I want to save you."

Outside, in the Jeep, Greg gunned the engine. Jake heard it.

"We're running out of time." He was getting tense and angry, losing his battle with frustration. Everything was against him—fate, the fire, Jennie. He felt his patience burning like a short fuse. "If you were here, I'd only worry. I'd be twice as likely to make a mistake, maybe get someone killed. I need to know you're safe."

"Then we understand each other. I need the same thing."

He hit the doorframe with the flat of his hand, uttering an ugly expletive. Looking down the valley toward the mountains and the path the fire would take, his voice was tight. He knew he was risking tearing them apart by asking for something Jennie might not be able to give. But he wasn't asking anymore.

"We're out of time. Ten minutes, Jennie. That's how long you have to pack." He tried to say her name again, make her turn and look at him. "Don't make me carry you out," he said as the screen slammed behind him.

For a bleak moment Jennie stared at the room around her. Ten minutes.

He wanted her to let him go, to leave when he was in danger. It went against everything she stood for. If only she'd expressed herself better, argued from a different angle. But she could waste her life on ifs, and she only had ten minutes.

She heard the engine of the Jeep being revved again in the drive, and the minutes crowded in around her—nine, eight. Her gaze lit on the bookshelves and her volumes of scrapbooks. Her entire career was pasted in those books. Could she take them all? And Karen's tapes—she had to take them. Without realizing it, she was clutching one already.

She had ten minutes to summarize a life, to leave her home—to leave the man she loved in the hands of fate.

He leaned against the fender of the Jeep, feeling the itch of dust, heat, and sweat mixing under his collar. Greg pumped the gas lightly when the engine sputtered. Jake peered at the house, his eyes unreadable, his arms crossed.

It was hellish in the sun. No air moved. A haze hung over the valley, making heat dance on grass that never bent. Jake felt just as brittle, waiting as the one thing that could make his life complete went up in smoke.

Jennie Cisco was a woman who wouldn't be pushed. He'd just pushed her. He didn't have time for calculated moves anymore, for winning her with steadiness and passion. The fire was forcing his hand. Maybe he could make promises about working with the computer, staying back from the lines in the future. But they'd sound hollow now. He would meet this fire head on, and they both knew it. Would she be waiting for him when it was over?

Greg cleared his throat twice, and Jake suspected he was trying to work up the nerve to tell him the time was up. Jake knew it. He ground his teeth audibly and counted to ten. Was she going to make it any harder? If she didn't move her little behind across the porch in half a minute, he was going to have to go in there and bodily—

The screen door opened. She set her guitar case on the porch, then disappeared back inside.

He went in after her. Because time was running out, he told himself, because he had to see her once more.

She had a suitcase spread open on the sofa. It contained very few clothes: a pair of jeans, a pair of slacks, a couple of blouses, some lingerie—champagne silk. Jake knew the feel of it as well as she did, remembered the way the panties whispered across the downy hair on her legs, heard the sigh of a camisole landing on the floor at her feet.

A handful of tapes clattered into the case. Music

notebooks followed, the kind he'd found her hunched over one evening, scribbling in at the piano. He'd kissed the back of her neck. They almost hadn't made it up the stairs.

Now she stood on the spot where they'd last made love, where tears and sweat and all her vulnerability had been laid bare to him, where there'd been no barriers at all.

She clicked the latches of the suitcase firmly shut and looked up. He held the door open for her. Setting the case beside her guitar, she looked out over the ranch.

"That's it?" he asked, nodding toward the one bag.

That was it. A lifetime packed in a suitcase. When it came right down to it, Jennie knew there weren't many essential things in life. Jake was one of them, and he was sending her away.

He brushed his thumbs across her cheekbones, watching her eyes darken, shimmering and wet. He wanted to drag her to him but knew she'd crumble if he did.

Her fingers found his face in a blur of tears, and she smiled. "Don't get burned."

"I already have." His eyes were as turbulent as the black plume on the horizon. He had so many questions to ask, but neither of them would have the answers until this was over.

"Promise me," she whispered brokenly. Then she was in his arms, their kiss desperate, eternal. She felt the power in his body, so alive, yet so easily snuffed out. He'd given her life again. He couldn't lose his. He'd be there when she returned—he had to be, she decided. There were only so many good-byes a heart could take.

Jake drew away first. As long as she was safe and

wanted him when the danger was over, then he could ask her the question he'd been wanting to ask for so long. "I love you," he said. "Don't forget."

She nodded, her voice all but gone.

He helped her into the front seat of the Jeep, fit himself in back. Greg made a U-turn in the drive and headed toward the trees and the mountain road. He stopped to drop Jake at a crossroads, where men with machinery were congregating to make a last stand against the fire.

Jake didn't say good-bye. He walked down the road, unknotting the bandanna around his neck. There were only so many good-byes a heart could take.

The motel was a series of numbered orange doors set in cinder block. Her room was chilled by an overanxious air-conditioner wheezing under a window. Jennie turned it off by force of habit. On the road she couldn't risk losing her voice to a cold. If motel rooms weren't damp, they were overheated and dry. She glanced at the signs of mildew in the bathroom and knew this one was never dry.

Gaudy flowered curtains sewn from some kind of plastic material matched the flowered bedspread on the double bed. Pendulous table lamps of harvest gold, a telephone, a Bible, a TV chained to its stand, and a brochure for satellite movies were all the room contained. It was as familiar as stepping back in time, she thought.

Jennie wanted to lie down. She wanted to take a long walk somewhere and exhaust herself. She wanted Jake, and she wanted him banished to a pedestal in her memory so he would never change, never be hurt. She'd thought she was protecting him from loving an idol. It was herself she'd been shielding. She'd known since the night on the veranda when she'd dared him to make love to her that nothing would ever hurt her as much as Jake's leaving. And nothing ever had.

Her guitar was at the foot of the bed. A closet full of empty coat hangers gaped at her, skeletons of anonymous travelers, like her. Welcome back, Jennie Cisco. Back on the road that led everywhere but home.

She dragged out her guitar and ran through a song. Her throat was too tight. The music kept blurring. She'd written the song for Jake, and he might never hear it. She flipped on the TV, hoping it would drown out the crying, the way the dark hid tears and the past buried mistakes.

Sometime later she fell asleep, awoke, knew Jake wasn't beside her, cried, and slept again, dreaming about a broad-shouldered man walking across her valley. She was riding Glaze down the mountain, shouting, but the man in the cowboy hat never heard her. He kept on walking.

Morning came, sunlight fighting its way through cracks in the curtains. Jennie's whole body ached, from the bed or the crying, she didn't know. She drew the curtains apart to gaze on the dusty drive, the highway passing her by, the telephone pole with a homemade poster flapping on it.

She called her parents before they heard about the worsening fire on TV. Anyone would have done the same, but it was Jake's concern for Shauna she thought of, his tenderness and caring.

She called Harbring's and checked on Glaze. Close to Owens Lake, he'd be safe.

She called her manager, Phil Summers, and tried to leave a cheerful message on his machine. "For the time being, you can nag me at the following number . . ."

Then she ran out of busyness, and the gaudy, cheerless room closed in and she was as homesick as she'd ever been. Were the windows still open at the house? Was the refrigerator on, the generator running? Someone should know about the nozzle on the propane tank attached to the stove. Someone should have given her time to close up.

She picked up the phone. It took a minute to remember her own number. She let it ring. She could hear it echoing in the empty house; pictured the table the phone sat on, waiting for someone to pick up. After twenty or thirty rings, she hung up. Her heart was pounding, and sweat trickled down her back. She'd been waiting, praying, for Jake to answer. What would she have said if he had? They'd said it all.

The homesickness lingered. No matter what happened, *El Dobro* was as good as gone. No miracle could make it stay the same if Jake wasn't there.

"Dammit!" She'd slammed the phone down so hard, she'd broken a nail. She was crying again, her face puffy, her eyes rubbed red. For some reason Jake hadn't minded seeing her that way. What would he think if he saw her falling apart again? What did she think?

"First of all, self-pity isn't going to bring him back," she said out loud. And sheer ego wasn't going to let her give up now. Pride had gotten her through living in a thousand motel rooms like the one she was in.

Digging through her suitcase, she found a small carryall full of toiletries. Years of touring had taught her to take the minimum she needed to get by, and she'd packed the cosmetics bag without thinking. She sat on the bed, her legs tucked under her, and sawed away with an emery board, staring blankly out the window. She had to do something to start over, to keep herself from going totally stir crazy.

Dry, crackling, and faded from the constant sunlight, the poster flapped against the pole. It was an advertisement for the fund-raiser for burned-out families at the school gym Saturday night. Two days away, she realized.

"Potluck in the basement afterward," she read. "Bring dish to pass." She picked up the phone and made another call.

The canvas awning blocked the sun like a big umbrella, casting rectangular shadows on the worktable. Every other tent at *El Dobro* was being dismantled, equipment carted off in trucks. They were bugging out. The Jennie he'd met ten days earlier would have been thrilled, Jake thought.

He put her out of his mind until the phone in the house rang again. He wondered who could be calling, and cursed the idiotic notion that it was she. Just thinking about the sound of her voice made his heart beat faster and his pulse trip. Maybe he should answer the damn thing. He was halfway to the house when it stopped. He scowled blackly and returned to the portable computer he'd borrowed for fieldwork. It was pointless. He'd seen everything the data could show him. "Burt!"

"Yeah, Jake?"

"Can you get me on the next chopper? I want to see it from the air. Tell 'em we'll pick up the humidity detectors Glen's crew left behind."

It was a logical enough excuse for mapping out how the fire would hit Jennie's place. There was a heavy stand of pines at the end of the valley, with a clearing in the center. Solid trees would've slowed the fire better. But unless God brought the rain first and the wind second, Jake would have to work with what he had. It looked as if this forest would be his last stand.

"Ten minutes," Eileen Wesson announced as she knocked on Jennie's dressing room door. She smiled fondly, as if she'd known Jennie would see the error of her ways and come around eventually.

Jennie sorted through her clothes. There was a blouse the color of bleached seashells mixed with fine silk strands of gold. It was cut to fall from one shoulder, and would set off her dark skin and hair perfectly. A pair of pleated linen slacks went with it. She pulled on the blouse as a local band crashed through its final chords onstage and was met with thunderous applause.

They've got mothers, fathers, and every relative in Lone Pine behind them, Jennie thought. But would the audience be more skeptical when the infamous, out-of-practice Jennie Cisco stepped on stage? She glanced uncomfortably at Eileen. At least this woman seemed to like her. "Quite a crowd, huh?"

"We doubled ticket sales in two days, thanks to you." She patted Jennie on the arm. "If you'd given us a little more notice, we might have tripled them. You're a godsend."

"Thanks," Jennie replied. At the moment it was all she could do to remember the order of her songs and forget how many times she'd flubbed them in practice. Too late to worry now, she told herself. She'd just have to live out that old show-biz maxim and go on with the show.

She picked up her guitar and motioned for Eileen to lead the way. "Hope the lions are hungry tonight."

Eleven

It roared like a train, a tornado, consuming oxygen, creating cinders. Tongues of flame devoured the horizon. The crackle of dry twigs and branches snapping, the sputter of sap boiling and popping in living branches. When he got near it, it was like a wall, a palpable barrier of heat that made the hair on his neck stand up. He drew thick air through the bandanna and into his lungs. The entire landscape looked watery through heat waves and tears of sweat.

Jake's clothes stuck to him like heavy skin. He'd been soaked in sweat within half an hour, and there'd been no getting dry after that. The wind had arrived with a vengeance Saturday afternoon, and the fire was totally out of hand. Forecasting was over. He and the men assigned to him chopped scrub and used axes to break the hard, dry ground. A puny string of human beings drawing the line, daring the dragon to step across.

Jake yelled, "Bump up," and the men took a step forward and kept digging. Fighting the fire now was a matter of containment and direction, and constantly keeping in mind where they were in relation to the roads—which were only dirt tracks that wound through the mountains for trucks carrying food, water, and medical supplies.

Back at the road, Jake ate a plate of food someone handed to him. Perching on a tailgate, he stared blankly ahead. He'd need his strength; they'd be fighting all night. The real nightmare was yet to come; keeping track of personnel in the dark was a bitch. The wind picked up, prickling over his skin. It was going to be one hell of a fight.

"Greg?"

"Hey, boss. Catching some chow?"

"I want you to take a message to Ed Kohodas. I need a few men assigned to me. I've got an idea."

Within half an hour they were in a wood positioned between two fields of grass. Jennie's ranch was at the end of one of those fields, the fire at the end of the other, the wood smack in the center. It was made up of lodgepole pines and Douglas firs. Although those particular trees were hard to burn, they were too well spaced for Jake's liking. The wind whistled through them as Greg, Burt, Joe, and a half dozen hand-picked men stood side by side, exhausted from three hours of digging, and clearing dead wood with chain saws. The radio on Jake's hip clattered with static. "Fire coming your way. Evacuate position. Evacuate."

"I can see it," Jake answered as a line of fire swept over the field toward them. Maybe their work would slow it down until the smoke jumper Jake had ordered dumped retardant on it.

"I said evacuate, Kramer!" the voice on the radio ordered.

"It's coming from the east. We see it. We're going into the woods."

"Not north! There's a branch of fire to the north, and it's burning your way. Get out of there now!"

There was no time to figure out how the wind had played its trick. The fire was circling around them like pincers.

"This way!" Jake shouted. The men scrambled through the vegetation, calling each other's names in an assigned buddy system, until they reached a clearing in the center, a hidden pasture of dry grass with mists of gray smoke billowing across it.

Jake counted the men around him and outlined the evacuation procedures. The fire was coming through scrub and young trees to the north. It was also closing in from the east. They had to get across the clearing to the southwest, into the pines on the far side, then out onto Jennie's land. From there they'd reach the road, where a truck would pick them up. "Okay, go!" They broke as if from a football huddle and started as one across the field.

It seemed to hit all of them separately. Each man stopped at a different spot as he saw it. Under the smoke curling around the far side of the clearing were sparks, then flames. The fire had made a complete circle, racing around the grass fields to cut them off.

"Get your fire shelters out. Now!" The men were already unpacking the yellow Nomex shields, four-by-six-foot aluminum covers they'd huddle under while the fire burned around them. "Where's that damn chopper?" Jake shouted to no one.

"Guess we'll see if these things really work," Greg said softly beside him.

Jake gave him a baleful look. "Sorry to get you into this. It was my battle."

"Oh, I dunno," Greg said, "I like her too." He grinned boyishly and crouched down. "Instead of us being around a campfire, the campfire will be around us. Now I know what a marshmallow feels like."

"Greg, would you shut up?" Jake muttered absently, counting every man safe inside his shield. Then he pulled the material over his head, holding it closed with clenched hands. It could be a miserable way to die, he thought. And Shauna would hear the details, no matter how her mother tried to spare her. And so would Jennie.

Jennie. He'd lost her ranch, driven her away, and, worst of all, he'd never really convinced her he loved her. He wanted to think of the best things they'd shared, but all he could think was, "I'm sorry, Jennie," as the wind whipped the fire across the clearing.

Jennie tried to remember the order of the new songs sprinkled among the old. "Just My Luck to Love a Cowboy" and "Karen's Song."

"I think that's your cue," Eileen said, proud of her lingo.

She was scared. It wasn't only the butterflies and the lack of practice; it was a clammy chill, bone deep, an erratic rhythm of her heart that made it hard to breathe, a sense of impending disaster. Something was terribly wrong, but she was minutes away from walking out on stage, and the feeling was so mixed in with all the other fears and the promises she'd make if only Jake could be there.

Jennie took a deep breath and counted to ten. She took a seat on the stool set on center stage, felt the heat of the lights, and listened to the unabashed ravings of the emcee.

"And now, one of the greatest singer-songwriters of our time . . ."

"Thanks for giving me something to live up to,"

she thought wryly, laughing it off as the curtain parted. Knowing it was too late to flee, she launched into a song by rote. When it was finished, the applause stunned her back to consciousness. She'd made it. One down and she wouldn't count how many left to go. She wiped her damp palms on the knees of the linen pants, managed a weak thanks, and began another number. Things were actually going well.

After four songs Jennie moved to the piano and adjusted the microphone, flipping her braid over her shoulder. The crowd even cheered at her trademark gesture. Time to say a few words during a pause in the action, she decided. The butterflies inside her fluttered back to life, their wings tickling her throat like birds in a chimney. "Whew!" she exclaimed, wiping the perspiration on her upper lip. "Is it warm in here, or is it just me?" The audience roared its agreement. The thin line of windows below the roof did little to vent the heat.

"As you know, it's been a while since I performed. Hope I'm not as rusty as this piano." They all laughed. She smiled. She was reaching out to people again. She was helping. If only Jake could see her. The thought pricked like a needle.

She was into the opening bars of "Montana," counting her blessings, when she heard her own voice singing, "Home, home, home . . ." At the motel she'd questioned whether she should sing it for people who'd lost theirs. But home was anywhere your loved ones were. Hands clasped, the family in the front row knew that, she realized. Missing Jake, Jennie knew it too.

Soon Jennie had won over the entire crowd. And, amazingly, it had won her over. She'd been wrong to forget the incredible love an audience could radiate. It didn't only take from her, it gave in return.

She sang "Karen's Song," then "Daybreak." It was like a furnace in the room, and no matter how the perspiration trickled down her back, or how long and loudly the audience applauded, she couldn't stop thinking about Jake.

"This is the last song." There were some groans, cheers. "It's called, 'Just My Luck to Love a Cowboy.' " And while the melody carried out over the rows of people, while the lights touched her face with their heat, she felt as if she were sitting cross-legged on the sofa, playing for Jake. And while her throat tightened and the tears blurred everything, she imagined she was watching the set of his shoulders as he walked toward the crossroads alone, to fight a fire, to save her ranch. She should have thanked him. She would. She owed him as much. Lord, how she owed him.

The ovation was enormous. A mixture of relief, fear, and grief washed over her so strongly, she could barely nod and get up from the piano before making a fool of herself. There'd be no encore.

She made her way offstage, choking back tears. Phil Summers was standing there, as always. He'd been to every show since her debut in Greenwich Village many years before. He was such a fixture, she collapsed in his arms without thinking of questioning his presence. Then she remembered she'd told him about the benefit over the phone. "Get me out of here," she said.

"In a few minutes, sweetheart." He patted her back and hugged her protectively. He'd get her through this, minute by minute. If she'd forgotten anything about touring, she should have remembered that.

"You did fine," he said.

She breathed a sigh of relief. "Thanks. I'm so glad you're here."

"What's a manager for?"

Phil went with her to the potluck reception after the show. The noise level in the school basement was horrendous. Logic kept telling Jennie an empty motel room was all that awaited her if she bowed out early, but she couldn't shake the tension gripping her, the feeling of being trapped.

She caught Phil watching her from across the room and made her way over. "Why are you standing back here? Don't tell me"—she held up her hand to silence his reply—"you're counting the gate."

"You wound me. Is that all you think I care about? But I'd say they cleared fifty thou easy. If everything's donated, that is."

"I always thought your name should be Phil S. Stein, as in philistine. This is about helping, not making money." She affectionately wound her arm through his. "Quite a crush of people, though."

"Anything for a good tuna casserole."

She rolled her eyes at him. "Thanks for the vote of confidence. I'd really like to go now, Phil. How about it?"

He nodded.

Leaving through a back door, they walked outside.

"Forgive me if I'm nagging, but it wouldn't hurt to know if this performance means you're coming back to the real world."

"I want to do an album, Phil. I have some new material, Karen's songs and mine. You heard some of them tonight."

"So welcome back." He put an arm around her shoulders and gave her a squeeze. "What about touring?"

"Phil!"

He put his hands up in self-defense. "Just asking. After all, I am your manager, the man who knows what's best for you. And making records means touring to promote them; otherwise, why bother?"

"I'll let you know."

They walked on, the night cool, due to a stiff wind and a misty rain. Jennie looked toward the mountains. "My ranch could be burning right now."

"So you rebuild."

"It's not just that." It's who's up there, she wanted to add.

"Then you love him, whoever he is." Fourteen years of working with Jennie had given Phil a leg up in the intuition department. As her manager, he knew Jennie had made him more money than ten clients. But the fatherly side of him said it was high time she was happy. "So what's Attila's real name?"

"Attila!"

"You told me last week your ranch had been invaded by Huns. One in particular."

"I did, didn't I? Jake Kramer."

"I take it he's stubborn enough to have earned the nickname?"

"Exactly."

"I take it he's also seen you at your best."

"I've played prima donna, threatened, screamed, pointed, stamped my feet, and ordered him off my land. I've even collapsed in tears."

Phil stopped to relight his cigar as the rain fell around them, pattering harder on the leaves of the trees. "And you think he doesn't love the real you."

It didn't hit her like a bolt of lightning; it dawned instead, like a sunrise. She'd never been protecting Jake from her star's image at all. "I've been a fool, haven't I?" She looked up at Phil, blinking back the rain, seized with a new fear. "I've wasted so much time, and we had so little."

"So why are you out here with me, walking in the pouring rain? Only people in love should do that."

Rain? She grabbed the lapels of his checked jacket. "It's pouring!"

"You want an umbrella?"

"The fire! It'll be put out by the rain! Don't you see?" She had to hurry. "I've got to get back to the ranch. Where are your car keys?"

Phil handed them over without an argument. "It's the red sports car. Your fireman might be busy, you know."

She called behind her as she rushed toward the parking lot. "He might need me." It was the only answer that mattered.

Twelve

The mountain was crawling with trucks and personnel. The road was rutted and bumpy, the compact car hard to control. Lights appeared out of nowhere around curves, and the wipers smeared as much as they cleared away. Oncoming trucks hogged the road, never expecting a little red car to be coming the other way. Jennie was forced to a stop more than once and told to go back. She ignored the warnings, prodded by the awful feeling that she should have come sooner. "Dammit, Jake, why did you send me away?"

She drove on, repeating to herself what Chick had told her. Jake was a careful man. He wouldn't take stupid risks to save her ranch.

Unless he loved her.

There was a moon, but the familiar road seemed unnaturally dark. When she realized the entire mountainside had been burned black, she clutched the wheel, ignoring the sinking feeling that was rapidly becoming a free fall into despair. With no foliage, and inches of rain predicted, there was the possibility of mud slides. Nothing was going to stop her before she got to Jake. Nothing.

She came around the last curve, consciously unclenching her fingers from the wheel. The ranch was still there, the house dark. But the bunkhouses were full of activity. They'd been converted to a medical-care post. She ran past the cots toward the first familiar face. "Greg! Where's Jake?"

The lanky redhead looked surprised to see her, but seemed to take it in stride. He wedged himself up off his cot on one elbow and nodded toward the private room at the back. Jennie walked toward it on suddenly trembling legs.

Chick's voice carried through the buzz of voices. "If we want your opinion we'll ask for it. Now, sit down!" If Jake was in there, Jennie heard no reply. A bad sign. Nobody back-talked Jake that way—except her.

She was about to step through the open door when Chick saw her. She could hear Jake mumbling and coughing. Gratitude coursed through her, because he was still alive, but it didn't loosen the coil of fear. How was he? Was he hurt? Was it her fault?

Chick blocked the door. "Stay out here. Jake can't be excited right now."

She automatically protested, but in a lowered voice. "I just want to see him. Is he hurt? Is he burned?" She searched the older man's eyes desperately, but they were unreadable.

"Would it matter if he was?" Although it was a genuine question, it hurt as much as if it had been an accusation. Did he really think she'd run away from his injuries?

"I just don't want him to be hurt, Chick, for his sake. I love him."

The older man accepted her answer with a solemn

nod. "Smoke inhalation, mostly. There's some burns on his hands. They were trapped for about ten minutes."

She felt a scream rising in her throat, and covered her mouth. She could see Chick reconsidering telling her. She got control of herself fast.

"From what I gather they were in a field, and the fire was quicker than they were. They used their fire shields." He explained how the material worked: "Like a raincoat that's fire-resistant. It's a hell of a way to sit and wait for a fire."

"Was anyone hurt?"

"Minor things—hands, smoke. Other than that, no, thank God. Most of these guys are just bone-tired, but Greg, there, he was in it." He nodded toward the redhead, who smiled, and waved with his bandaged hand.

Jennie turned back to Chick. She had to ask. "Was it my fault? Did he do this because of me?"

"I wondered that myself for a minute. But nobody can make Jake do what he doesn't want to. He's stubborn as an unbroken bronc, he is. Always was." Although he'd said it gruffly, he gave her a half-smile.

Jennie hugged him hard. "I'm just as stubborn, Chick. Let me see him."

"There's the chance of his going into shock."

"I won't talk. I won't say anything. Just let me sit beside him. I could hold the oxygen mask."

Chick considered the planks in the floor.

"He did as much for me once," she said softly.

Before he could answer, there was a commotion at the door of the bunkhouse; another exhausted fire fighter was being helped in. The bunkhouse was getting crowded.

"Why don't they take him to the main house? There's no more room in here," Jennie remarked.

"Jake's orders. Said no one was to set so much as a bootheel in there. If everything wasn't spotless when you got back, he'd skin 'em personally."

Jennie felt herself flush with feelings she couldn't name. That stubborn, foolish man! she thought. Didn't he know she loved him more than she'd ever loved this piece of land?

Her voice carried effortlessly to the end of the bunkhouse. "Get them into the main house, dammit! What do you think it's there for?"

Chick smiled at the startled medics. "You heard the lady. The main house is open." To Jennie, as he ran a hand through his short gray hair, he merely said, "Go on in."

Jake was sitting on the edge of the cot, an oxygen mask strapped to his face, both hands tightly gripping the edge of the thin mattress. He'd thought he heard her voice. He'd sat up so fast, he'd damn near blacked out. He was in the middle of cursing himself for hallucinating the one thing he wanted most, when she stepped in the door.

The sandals and mud-splattered white slacks were too stylish to be any nurse's uniform. The medics wore jeans or work pants. But she could be a nurse, he guessed. She probably was. He had an overwhelming urge to tell her to go tend the men who were more hurt than he.

So why was he scared stiff of looking up? Was he afraid of seeing *her*, or of being disappointed for the hundredth time? From the moment the chopper had flown them out of the field, he'd been praying she'd come. But she was doing a show in town; he'd heard about it on the radio. It didn't stop him from imagining her, hearing her voice at the oddest moments and jumping. Ironic what a brush with death would do to a man's perceptions—pointing out that what mattered most was the woman he'd sent away. Even if it was for her own good. Either way, he kept staring at the sandals, not wanting the dream to stop.

She could see the muscles bunched in his thighs and the tension in his shoulders. He looked as if he were about to run, as if it were taking all his strength just to sit and keep it bottled up, to keep his eyes on the floor.

She also knew the moment he realized it was she. There was a growing awareness in the room, something between them that had always been there. The tension rose by degrees, the decibel level of the voices outside dropping like a barometer before a storm. He didn't move, didn't say anything. He splayed his fingers once and gripped the bed again.

Just to get across the threshold, Jennie had to call upon everything she'd ever learned about stepping onto a stage when thousands of people were waiting. None of them had ever mattered as much as Jake.

He was so handsome. Uncompromisingly masculine, physically brawny, with a boyish thatch of straw-blond hair, dirty and smoky and mussed. Every time he'd been away and come back, she'd forgotten exactly how beautiful he was. Even at that moment he made her heart pound. The slam of her physical reaction mingled with the cold, absolute fear that she might have lost him.

She still could. She had to make him stay.

She lowered herself onto the cot beside him and waited. There were black spots on his shirt and burns on his arm, red circles from flying cinders that had landed and been shaken off with a quick curse. The burns on the backs of his hands were uglier, angry red and purple, and smeared with some kind of salve. He was breathing shallowly into the mask, his gaze fixed intently on the floor. The lines in his face were deeper, and he looked more tired than she'd ever seen him—and in more pain. She couldn't tell if it was from the burns or her presence. Either way, she was to blame.

The noise in the other room was a constant murmur. Rain spattered and pounded on the wooden roof. The wind whistled through the boards and across the silent gulf between them.

Then he looked at her, his eyes startlingly blue in a face darkened by smoke and sweat. He was waiting. Jennie felt tears well up, and forced them back. She couldn't sit there and cry over him. Pride, she thought, everyone has pride.

So she smiled instead, a stiff, off-center smile, as she wiped a strand of hair from his damp forehead. She had to force herself to go no further, had to resist skimming her fingers down his face, fight the urge to touch the deep lines around his eyes. "You're a mess," she said, chiding him as she might a little boy who'd lost his comb. "You could use a shower."

He moved to take off the oxygen mask.

"No, not yet," she said, seized with unexplainable panic. She touched the plastic with her fingertips, coaxing it back into place, rushing to say what she'd come to say. "I love you, Jake. If I've been afraid, made mistakes, or hurt you, I'm sorry." She broke off when her voice cracked.

Jake took one more breath, then held the mask in his lap.

"How did you get up here?" His voice was deep, ragged. His hard blue eyes gave nothing away. Jake half suspected she saw anger there, but he couldn't give an inch or the dam would break. "How?"

"You know how stubborn I can be." As a smile,

hers didn't really work. The eyes were too scared, the corners of her mouth taut and stretched. Did she know how those rare moments of vulnerability got to him? Did she have any idea how she tore him up? "Let me stay, Jake. We don't have to talk right now."

He dragged in more oxygen, while she sat with her hands in her lap, so prim except for the tantalizing bit of skin where her blouse had slipped off her shoulder. He wondered if she could feel his breath on her bare skin, and it made him ache in the only place where he hadn't ached until she'd walked in. "Do you remember what we almost did in this room?"

Vividly, she thought. He'd carried her in, tossed her down, and, when she'd expected the worst, he'd taken care of her, getting her oxygen. They kept it away from fire areas, he explained once. In its pure form it was highly combustible. Like the two of them.

She touched him tenderly, her shaking fingers closing over his hand on the mask. "Except you were holding me then."

"Jennie."

"I love you."

"Say it again."

"I love you."

The dam was breaking, and he was powerless to stop it. When the tears rolled down her cheeks and something inside him said, *Hold her, you idiot, touch her now,* it was all over. He couldn't have stopped it if he'd tried.

With one motion he tugged her off balance, back onto the cot, his body hard against hers, branding her softness into his skin for all time. "Say it again, Jennie. I need to hear it."

But he didn't give her a chance to answer. She had to be his. Completely. There was no way he could stay behind the lines she drew. He was shaking inside and out. He knew he was holding her too tightly, but he couldn't stop the words from tumbling out, no matter how stripped his throat, how raw his voice. He was drawing his lines now, and he wanted—no, *needed*—her to step across of her own free will. She had to know the stakes.

"When I give, I don't hold back. It's everything, Jennie. I want it all. I can't handle half a love. I can't carry it by myself. I need a woman who knows what she wants. Who wants *me*, so there's no doubt, because doubts will tear a man up inside faster than anything else.

"I need a woman who's as stubborn as I am, and hell-bent on making this work. Unfortunately, I have no choice about the woman. It's you, and it always will be. If you want me, Jennie, say yes. Tell me if it's going to work or if I should get out of here and never look back."

He wiped the hair from her face. Then he was stroking her cheek, the dampness by her earlobe where a tear had run. It was a mistake. She had skin like tawny satin, too easy to touch. He could have gotten lost in those caramel-brown eyes, he thought, especially when they held a spark of memory and desire, of intimacy shared, of nights when they'd twined exactly the way they were now.

Her body had molded to his; her arms were around his waist. Her long, delicate fingers, which had once reminded him of darting, angry birds, kneaded the muscles in his back, and her thighs brushed his.

"I should have told you I loved you sooner," she said softly, then smiled up at him.

He chuckled, and the exertion brought on a coughing fit.

Jennie disengaged herself quickly and clamped

the mask to his face. She stroked his back with her other hand, touching the body she'd relegated to memory for too many empty nights. When his breathing returned to normal, she said, "Now, what's this about your risking your life for a worthless clod of earth and some outbuildings? This clapboard tinderbox doesn't even have electricity!"

He felt a grin tugging at his mouth, and spoke out of the other side of the mask. "That's okay. I've got my battery-operated computer now."

"Jake Kramer, you bully your way onto my ranch, into my house, and into my life, and you think I'm going to let you get away with using some other damned computer? I fight for the things I love. You saw how I fought for this ranch, and I don't love it nearly as much as I do you!"

"Then tell me again," he said, lowering the mask. "You're not the only one who needs to be convinced, Jennie." He leaned back, a challenging twinkle in his eyes.

Somehow she'd always known he'd sit back and wait for her to come to him. She resisted out of sheer habit, lifelong ingrained stubbornness. Until she realized surrender didn't always mean losing. "I'll show you," she whispered, placing one knee on the bed while her fingers slid around to the back of his collar.

The deep, slow breath he took had nothing to do with a need for oxygen, although suddenly he felt starved for it.

She said something softly against the shell of his ear. She could turn him inside out, doing that, and she knew it. Night after night he'd told her so. The mask clattered to the floor, and he knew it was his own damn fault. He never should have pushed Jennie.

He let her kiss the corner of his mouth, determined not to move while she teased his lips with hers. His control lasted all of ten seconds, until she bit his lower lip. His arms were around her in a crushing embrace, and they tumbled backward onto the cot. Their mouths met in a hungry commingling of tenderness and passion, moistness and heat, seeking forgiveness and finding nothing but love, again and again and again. The more he clutched her to him, the more willingly she came, her smile wide and triumphant.

He tasted awful, like tar. And his hands in her hair carried the aroma of ointment and medicine. His clothes were stiff with smoke, and his hair, when she ran her hands through it, was clumped and thick. None of it mattered. In minutes his mouth tasted familiar and tangy, intoxicatingly male—thoroughly Jake.

And their memories came to life, the tiny bites he ran along her collarbone, the way she pecked at the tip of his nose. He pushed the blouse off her shoulder and worried her bare skin with love play, working his way back up to bury his head against her neck. A whiff of perfume brought reality home.

"I must stink to high heaven."

She laughed, low and sultry. "Let me kiss you again and I'll tell you about it."

He ran his hand up and down her arm, satin, skin, then satin. "Did I tell you that you look beautiful? Never more beautiful than tonight."

She smiled a seductive smile that made his eyes go dark, and he moved his hand to her breast. He withdrew it again. "What's wrong?" she asked.

"I don't want to ruin this blouse. I've never seen it before."

"I wore it onstage."

Yes, he thought, something classy and chic, with just a few strands of gold. A designer number. "There are things you need that I can't give you, Jennie."

"You can't mean money."

"I mean crowds. You deserve them. You've earned the right to be cheered." He'd seen the way she'd lit up, singing for a handful of men. She was a star, and she needed to shine. "How did it go tonight?"

"Good."

"That's all?"

"There was a ten-minute standing ovation at the end. A lot of money was raised."

"How did *you* feel?"

"Scared. Happy. Not bad, considering." He hadn't been there. It had made all the difference.

"You enjoyed being in the spotlight again."

"As a matter of fact, yes," she said shortly. She sensed where he was leading. "I'd be a fool to trade you for success, Jake. Two hours and it's over and they all go home to people they love, and I get on a bus headed for somewhere else."

She touched his face, and her hands ran over his shoulders, his chest. She had to force herself to stop and just rest her cheek against his before she could speak again. "I want to have you to come home to."

He swallowed thickly. Her hands knew how to excite him, but her words were more than he could handle. "Are you sure that's what you want?"

She couldn't push for commitment; he had to give it freely. "There are a lot of things I want. For instance, do you think I really give a damn about this blouse?" She picked up his smoke-blackened palm and held it to her breast.

He felt her skin's heat through it, and the erect nub of her breast. His heart was hammering. "Maybe we shouldn't. It looks new."

"I could take it off." Now the dare was hers. She got up to close the door softly, and with a suggestive sway, walked toward him.

He stood to meet her. He was so happy, it made him light-headed. He'd never felt so eager, and, dammit, the room was spinning just because she was in his arms. "You sang my song?" he asked, " 'Just My Luck—' "

"I was going crazy without you." He swayed heavily in her arms. "Jake?"

"Huh?"

"Where's the oxygen?"

"I dunno."

"Jake, if you fall down I can't pick you up!" She forced him back onto the bed, only to find herself trapped beneath him.

"You're not going anywhere," he said with a growl.

"I wasn't planning on it." That was a fib. She'd been meaning to run for a doctor.

There was a loud knock on the door, and a man with a black bag entered. Jennie almost cheered until she realized the position she was in. She unwound Jake's arms from around her, rolled him to the side, and wriggled upright.

Jake sat up and pulled Jennie to his side. His immediate recovery was stunning, but she guessed it was superficial. He began with a blunt hello, then launched into a rapid-fire interrogation. "Have you seen to everyone else? How are the men? How's the fire?"

"Yes, all fine, and it's out," the doctor said, pulling up a stool. "I'd like to take your blood pressure." He gave Jennie a glance, but she was powerless to move any farther down the bed. Jake's hold on her waist kept her tightly by his hip.

The doctor sighed and wrapped Jake's arm as

best he could to take his blood pressure. He pumped the rubber balloon and watched the needle bounce as it fell. "Any light-headedness?"

"No." "Yes." They both answered at once, trading dirty looks.

"He was dizzy a few moments ago," Jennie offered.

Jake denied it with a one word expletive.

The doctor handed Jennie the oxygen mask. "Keep it on him, keep him flat on his back, and don't let him out of that bed until morning. Got that?"

"Yes, sir," she replied obediently.

Jake contradicted their opinion of his health by letting loose a more imaginative string of curses. The doctor was already out the door.

"You lie here quietly," she murmured soothingly.

"Like hell I will. I want to see how Burt and Greg are doing. And Joe and—"

With two hands flat against his chest, she pushed him back. "No way, buster. I've got my orders."

An aide came in with a bowl of water and a washcloth. Jennie spent the next twenty minutes dabbing at the small burns of Jake's arms and applying salve. She stretched across him to wipe the dirt from his forehead, and he caught her braid as it swung over her shoulder. While she was otherwise occupied he worked the ribbon off with one hand, unbraiding her hair slowly.

"What are you doing?"

"What do you think? What's this?" he asked when he encountered another obstacle.

"Something to keep it neater." She sat back and undid the second rubber band at the top of her braid.

"You always perform with it braided?"

"Always."

"What about on your album covers?"

"All five."

She was absently fluffing her mane of wild hair, while they contemplated each other as the rain drummed on the roof.

"Then I'm the only one who sees you this way." He wanted promises, exclusivity. If he had to share her with a million others, he wanted a part of her that was his alone. "Promise me."

"It's a deal."

He closed his eyes and breathed more easily. Something crossed his mind, a sadness, a memory. The fire. He shook it off and opened his eyes. She was sitting patiently, like the dream that replaces a nightmare. He squeezed her hand.

"Was it bad?"

"Like pitching a pup tent in hell." He couldn't really describe it, the sound, the smell, the heat, the responsibility eating him up for the men he'd brought. And the knowledge that Jennie standing on a veranda, with a guitar and a suitcase, was the last image he'd have of her.

She didn't press him to put it into words. He was definitely groggy. She smiled every time he opened his eyes, said less and less, and felt his grip on her wrist go slack. His men were all right, the fire was over, and she was there. Soon he'd be asleep.

They were home.

Thirteen

It was dawn. A dusky pink haze filtered over the valley. The cool air touched the warm earth, and mist floated over the grass. The ranch was deserted now, all traces of the firemen cleared away.

They'd been sleeping in the bedroom off the veranda, huddling together during the chilly nights. Jake had chosen it, with the screen their only door.

Gingerly he disengaged himself from their embrace, trying not to wake her. He stood in the doorway, slipping on an old pair of jeans that rode low on his hips, and looked out at the encroaching mountains, sturdy guardians of the valley. They'd watch over Jennie while he was gone.

A surprising sensation of homesickness hit him all at once. He'd miss the place more than he'd ever missed his apartment in Butte. He felt as if he belonged here. The feeling was mixed with guilt. For four days they'd been loving—sharing a bedroom, long breakfasts, afternoon walks, tending Glaze. Now his week of sick leave was almost up. He'd be going soon, and he hadn't told Jennie.

"Jake?" Unfailingly, her sleepy, husky voice stirred him. He turned and leaned against the doorframe and just looked at her. She was naked, as she'd been the first time he'd seen her, her hips outlined under the sheet. Her skin was rosy and golden in the half light. But this time no braid rested on the flushed tip of her breast. Hair outlined her tawny oval face, wild and black and loose. His physical reaction to her hadn't dimmed one bit.

She stretched languidly, her eyes half open, watching him. He had one leg crossed over the other, making her think of how those legs felt with hers wrapped around them. In the fading haze of sleep she remembered their fiendish, demanding loving in the night, when he woke with a start and she touched him softly, and they met on that field of fire, driving each other beyond memory to a time before.

His back was so broad, almost filling the doorway, and she itched to run her hands across it, press her nails into it. "Come back to bed; it's cold out there."

The nubs of his nipples were tight among the swirls of golden hair, his arousal an unmistakable answer to her request. He walked over to the bed, and she touched him, not shyly, running her hand up the denim, watching his chest move with one deep breath, his abdomen tighten.

"For a man on sick leave you're mighty healthy." Her lazy grin elicited no smile. A chill ran through her that had nothing to do with the cold. He'd told her he loved her countless times, but he'd never promised to stay. "Jake?"

He sat on the bed, looking toward the wall. When he remembered how warm the bed was and how well the contours of their bodies molded in sleep, he couldn't think beyond spending one more morning in bed with her. He'd found out so much in four days, how love got deeper and deeper and things could still be left unsaid. "I need to be getting back."

Jennie tried to take his words at face value. Of course he had to get back. The question was, "How long will you be away?"

"There's a fire in Idaho."

He hadn't answered her question. She ran a fingernail down his spine. He straightened but kept his eyes on the adobe wall. "Jennie, I'm trying to talk."

"And I'm trying to make you stay."

He looked at her. "That wouldn't be hard."

"What do I have to say? I love you? I do. I've said it so many times over the last few days."

"When you came to me Saturday night, I told you I wanted everything, all your love. But I know I can't push you without losing you," he said.

"Commitment, then." Her heart was pounding. Couldn't he see that was what she wanted? Hadn't she made it obvious? No, the present had been too precious, so they'd talked about everything except the future.

"I have to work, Jennie. My consulting can keep me in one place most of the year, but there's no getting around it; fire season is going to see me all over the map. I won't always be here when you need me."

"Did I say I objected to that?" Jennie carefully planned out loud. "I've been wondering myself if I won't need private time."

"You wouldn't mind my being gone?" He looked at her doubtfully.

She smiled lazily and poked him in the ribs. "I'm used to filling up my days—I have my own work to do. That's why I was wondering how you'd feel if I traveled too."

"How much?"

She plucked absently at the sheet. "A month in a studio in L.A. followed by an eight-week tour in the fall."

"Phil's idea?" Jake thought about the pudgy man in the checked suit with the horrible chewed-up cigars, and remembered the few words that had passed between them Sunday afternoon when he'd come to see Jennie's ranch. "Sticks and logs" had been his comment. But Jake knew there was no one he'd trust more to look after Jennie on the road. Phil's concern for her had come through loud and clear.

"His agenda, my idea," she corrected. "I enjoyed playing at the high school, Jake. The stage fright may never go away, but I like to share my music. Not doing that was one way of punishing myself for failing Karen, and punishing the world for the way everyone turned their backs on her. But I think I've learned I don't need to solve everyone's problems. I can just sing. Share. Besides, you've never seen me sing in public."

He smiled and felt proud for no reason he could think of. It really would be something to have her sing to him as she had that evening at her house— but with a thousand people listening. Hell, ten thousand, he decided. "I'd like that."

"You know"—she sat up suddenly—"if the summer's your busy season, and since it's one of the best seasons for touring, maybe we could go at the same time. Then we wouldn't miss each other so much."

"I'd rather know you're here when I'm not. That way we'd both have someplace to call at night."

"Call home?"

"Yeah."

They looked at each other for a long moment, both aware that a decision was being made in the joined silence.

He touched her abdomen lightly, trying to keep his gaze off the sheet bunched in her lap and the way her breasts reacted to the cold air. "If you keep touring, that means you'll stay on the Pill."

"For now." She kissed his palm and trod lightly with her next question. "But what about Shauna?"

"Visiting here, you mean?"

She nodded.

He pictured his little girl staying with him for more than a weekend. It was almost too much to hope for. But Jennie had taught him one or two things about fighting for what you love. "Get her a horse and she'll idolize you forever. She's at that age."

"We'll get you one, too, and we'll all go riding together."

Jake liked the idea almost as much as the happiness in Jennie's eyes. Life couldn't be this perfect, could it? he wondered. "You may find Shauna is all the children you want. She's, uh, headstrong."

"Like her father!" She laughed and put her hand on his chest. It stayed there, moving down slowly while she watched his eyes cloud with desire. "I think I can handle stubbornness."

"If I spend the summer fighting fires, and you tour this fall—"

"We'll have her come in late spring. After school is out. If you're only gone for a few days at a time, she could even stay with me, and we'd both be here waiting for you."

He nodded. It was all he could do, with the lump

in his throat. He ran a hand down her body, pausing to touch her in special places.

"You do that again and we may start another fire," she whispered.

"Then you'll marry me when I get back?"

She held his face in her hands, wondering if fear would always find its way into their happiness. He was coming back, but first he had to fight another fire. "Don't get hurt."

"I promise."

"Forever?"

"And ever. You think I'd risk losing this?" He kissed her gently, his lips moving over hers in their own sweet rhythm. "You still haven't answered my question."

"I thought I had." She kissed his nose. "Yes." She kissed his lips. "Yes." She kissed his neck, and he hugged her so fiercely, she began to pound him on the back. "I can't marry you if I can't breathe!"

"Sorry." Laughing, he tucked a strand of hair behind her ear.

They kissed long and slow, their words murmuring in the soft light as he lay her back on the bed. "I think Shauna will make a beautiful bridesmaid."

"So do I."

"Jake?"

"Shhh. The sun's coming up. Let's welcome the day right." It was no fantasy, but Jake knew he'd dream of this moment every night he was away.

Jennie knew how to touch him to make their loving go fast or to take it slow, but there was still so much to learn. Such as how she could love anyone as much as she loved him. Such as how his mouth on her breast made her heart double its beat one time, slow to a delicious pounding the next. How he could trail a line of kisses down to her waist, touching only the tiny hairs, never the skin. How she burned and shivered at the same time, his breath scattering love words and promises over the inside of her thigh.

Her skin was hot enough to match his. Her rapid breathing was interrupted by moans and words and pleas. They promised forever, but they knew that was a long way off. Right then, body to body, the inescapable reality was of him sinking inside her as she wrapped herself around him.

She curved her arms around his neck and touched her lips to the spot beneath his ear. He had a scar on his jaw. She'd have to ask him about it. But then he thrust, and she shuddered, and the thought vanished in a wave of sensation. The man she'd mistaken for a dream one morning was real, so real, so deep inside her, drawing out, then in, saying her name over and over again, the same way he said the word *love.*

Suddenly his arms went to her waist, pressing her to him. His whole body was taut, his face strained as he begged her not to move. "Is it dawn yet?"

She glimpsed the sky past his shoulder. They waited, breathing hard, looking into each other's eyes, until she whispered, "Now." And they moved together, the sun bursting over the horizon in startling rays of reds and golds, and behind closed eyes they both saw the dawn.

THE EDITOR'S CORNER

We have some deliciously heartwarming and richly emotional LOVESWEPTs for you on our holiday menu next month.

Judy Gill plays Santa by giving us **HENNESSEY'S HEAVEN**, LOVESWEPT #294. Heroine Venny McClure and a tantalizing hunk named Hennessey have such a sizzling attraction for each other that mistletoe wouldn't be able to do its job around them . . . it would just shrivel under their combined heat. Venny has come to her family-owned island to retreat from the world, not to be captivated by the gloriously handsome and marvelously talented Hennessey. And he knows better than to rush this sweet-faced, sad-eyed woman, but her hungry looks make him too impetuous to hold back. When the world intrudes on their hideaway and the notoriety in her past causes grief, Venny determines to free Hennessey . . . only to discover she has wildly underestimated the power of the love this irresistible man has for her.

Two big presents of love are contained in one pretty package in **LATE NIGHT, RENDEZVOUS**, LOVESWEPT #295, by Margaret Malkind. You get not only the utterly delightful love story of Mia Taylor and Boyd Baxter but also that of their wonderfully liberated parents. When Boyd first confronts Mia at the library where she works, he almost forgets that his purpose is to enlist her help in getting her mother to cool his father's affections and late-blooming romanticism. She's scarcely able to believe his tales of her "wayward" mother . . . much less the effect he has on her. Soon, teaming up to restrain the older folks, they're taking lessons in love and laughter from them!

Michael Siran is the star twinkling on the top of the brilliantly spangled **CAPTAIN'S PARADISE**, LOVESWEPT #296, by Kay Hooper. Now that tough,

(continued)

fearless man of the sea gets his own true love to last a lifetime. When Robin Stuart is rescued by Michael from the ocean on a dark and dangerous night, she has no way of knowing that it isn't mere coincidence or great good luck that brought him to her aid. Indeed, they are both deeply and desperately involved with bringing the same ruthless man to justice. Before love can blossom for this winning couple, both must face their own demons and find the courage to love. Join Raven Long and friends for another spellbinding romantic adventure as "Hagan Strikes Again!"

You'll feel as though your stocking were stuffed with bonbons when you read **SWEET MISERY**, LOVESWEPT #297, by Charlotte Hughes. Roxie Norris was a minister's daughter—but certainly no saint! —and she was determined to win her independence from her family. Tyler Sheridan, a self-made man as successful as he was gorgeous, owed her father a big favor and promised to keep an eye on her all summer long. But Tyler hadn't counted on Roxie being a sexy, smart spitfire of a redhead who would turn him on his ear. She is forbidden fruit, yet Tyler yearns to teach her the pleasures of love. How can he fight his feelings for Roxie when she so obviously is recklessly, wildly attracted to him? The answer to that question is one sizzling love story!

You'll love to dig into **AT FIRST SIGHT**, LOVESWEPT #298, by Linda Cajio. Angelica Windsor was all fire and ice, a woman who had intrigued and annoyed Dan Roberts since the day they'd met. Conflict was their companion at every meeting, it seemed, especially during one tough business negotiation. When they take a break and find a baby abandoned in Dan's suite, these two sophisticates suddenly have to pull together to protect the helpless infant. Angelica finds that her inhibitions dissolve as her maternal qualities grow . . . and Dan is as enchanted with her as he is

(continued)

filled with anxious yearning to make the delightful new family arrangement last forever. A piece of holiday cake if there ever was one!

There's magic in this gift of love from Kathleen Creighton, **THE SORCERER'S KEEPER**, LOVESWEPT #299. Never has Kathleen written about two more winsome people than brilliant physicist Culley Ward and charming homemaker Elizabeth Resnick. When Culley finds Elizabeth and her angelic little daughter on his doorstep one moonlit night, he thinks he must be dreaming . . . but soon enough the delightful intruders have him wide awake! Elizabeth, hired by Culley's mother to look after him while she's on a cruise, turns out to be everything his heart desires; Culley soon is filling all the empty spaces in Elizabeth's heart. But healing the hurts in their pasts takes a bit of magic and a lot of passionate loving, as you'll discover in reading this wonderfully heartwarming and exciting romance.

It gives me a great deal of pleasure to wish you, for the sixth straight year, a holiday season filled with all the best things in life—peace, prosperity, and the love of family and friends.

Sincerely,

Carolyn Nichols

Carolyn Nichols
Editor
LOVESWEPT
Bantam Books
666 Fifth Avenue
New York, NY 10103

THE DELANEY DYNASTY

Men and women whose loves and passions are so glorious it takes many great romance novels by three bestselling authors to tell their tempestuous stories.

THE SHAMROCK TRINITY